COFFEE, CREAM PIES, AND CRIMES

A Cape Bay Cafe Mystery
Book 11

HAPER LIN

This is a work of fiction. Names, characters, organizations, places, events, and incidents are either products of the author's imagination or are used fictitiously.

Coffee, Cream Pies, and Crimes

Copyright © 2023 by Harper Lin.

All rights reserved.

No part of this book may be reproduced, or stored in a retrieval system, or transmitted in any form or by any means, electronic, mechanical, photocopying, recording, or otherwise, without express written permission of the author.

www.harperlin.com

Chapter 1

"SMILE, FRAN!"

I looked up from watching my newest hire pull a shot of espresso to see Sammy Eriksen, my right-hand woman and probably the right half of my brain, holding her cell phone in my face. My first reaction was to make a face and pull back, which made Sammy make her own face.

"I can't use that." To her credit, Sammy didn't look annoyed with me for ruining her video yet again. Then again, Sammy only looked truly irritated in the rarest of circumstances. She smiled. "We'll try again."

"Fran?"

I turned to the teenager standing next to me and looking confused. She was holding an espresso cup in one hand and a milk-steaming wand in the other. The wand hovered over the espresso cup. Was she about to steam the coffee?

"Oh, nope!" I took the espresso cup from her and handed her the milk jug instead.

She smiled as the pieces clicked together, and she began steaming the right component of the latte.

I had recently hired a handful of new employees. I had Sammy and other experienced workers help me find competent, responsible part-timers who wanted to work a few hours each week in the Italian café. My family had run it since my grandparents came to Massachusetts from Italy nearly seventy-five years before. I paid well and offered flexible hours, but competition for summer employees was fierce in a beach town like Cape Bay.

For the teenaged crowd, working in a coffee shop a couple blocks from the beach wasn't one of the "cool" jobs they wanted to take. They tended to gravitate toward lifeguarding if their swimming skills were good enough or jobs directly on our small boardwalk if they weren't. Meanwhile, the relatively older adults looking for a little supplemental income tended to think we were too close to the beach for their comfort.

Somehow, despite all that, I'd managed to hire four new people to take some of the burden off my small existing crew. Chloe Patel and Daria Shah were high school students who were friends of my existing student employees, Becky and Amanda. Jessica Harris was an elementary school teacher looking for a summer job to earn a little extra cash. And Donna Williams was a friend of my other employee, Rhonda. Like Rhonda, she was a mom of teenagers who was looking for an excuse to get out of the house and a way to earn some spending money. Between them and everyone who had been there before I'd even taken over, I felt like we had a strong team to get through the busy tourist season.

Now that we were staffed up, Sammy had decided that it was time to step up our social media presence. She was filming a series of videos, profiling each of us who worked in the café. Despite my objections, she started with me, filming what seemed to be enough footage for a full-length documentary. She'd recorded me baking, fixing drinks, opening the café, closing it, baking at home, chatting with customers, teaching the new employees, and smiling at the camera what felt like a million times.

"You know, when I agreed to this, I thought you were talking about thirty seconds or something."

Out of the corner of my eye, I watched Chloe frothing the milk. She glanced over at me, and I nodded. She'd come in not knowing the difference between drip coffee and espresso or iced coffee and cold brew (although, to be fair, plenty of people who ordered them didn't know the difference either), but she had come a long way in her short few days of work. Her progress was slow but steady, and I was happy with that. "Okay, you can pour it now."

She looked nervous but put down the steaming wand. "Should I make a picture or something?"

"Don't worry about that yet. Just pour it in for now." Given how much her hand was shaking, I didn't think she could pour steadily even if she was ready to take on latte art. Dainty designs poured into the foam of our drinks were a signature of Antonia's Italian Café—named for my grand-mother—but it wasn't the end of the world if one drink didn't have one. Besides, this one was for me anyway.

She nodded and bent over the espresso cup to

pour in the milk. I stood beside her, watching, and gently touched her arm when there was enough. She stepped back and put the milk pitcher down, sighing as if the weight of the world was suddenly off her shoulders.

I picked up the latte and sipped it as she looked on with big eyes. I smiled. It was perfect.

"Look at me, guys!"

This time, I remembered what Sammy was doing and turned to her with a broad smile on my face.

"How's she doing, Fran?"

I turned my smile back to Chloe. "She's doing great! She's a coffee star in the making!" A delicate blush crept up her tan cheeks. I looked back at Sammy in case she had any other questions.

"That's perfect!" Sammy beamed at us. "Cut!" She tapped the phone and started fiddling with it.

I leaned over to Chloe. "I'm serious, you know. You're doing great."

The blush moved farther up her face. "Thanks."

"Why don't you go help Rhonda with the inventory?"

She nodded and went to join Rhonda in the back room.

I took another sip of my latte as Sammy came

over to show me her phone. My dark hair on her screen was a little fuzzy from the humidity, and a few strands had slipped out of the chignon I usually kept it in while I was working. My cheeks were flushed from leaning over steaming cups of coffee, and I had a smudge of flour on my forehead.

"Are you sure you want to use this?"

"Yes, absolutely." Sammy's blond ponytail bobbed as she nodded enthusiastically.

"At least it's just for social," I said. "People will know what to expect when they come in if nothing else."

Sammy giggled. "You look great! You don't need hair and makeup for a—" She stopped so suddenly that I looked toward the door to see if a celebrity or something had come in, but there was no one there. "—For a social media video."

"Are you okay?"

"Of course! Just lost my train of thought for a second! Now, let's get some footage of you baking and talking about what you like about it."

"I don't know—we have customers—"

Sammy cut me off with a gesture around the empty café. It was one of the few times at this time of year that things were quiet. Normally, we spent the lull frantically cleaning up before the next wave of customers came in, but with the additional staff we'd hired, we'd kept up during the rush. I simultaneously wondered why we hadn't hired more people sooner and wished we hadn't done so yet so that I had an excuse not to film anything else. I suddenly understood how my clients in my previous life as a New York City celebrity publicist must have felt when I made demand after demand of them.

I had no choice but to give in. "Okay, fine. What do you want me to make?"

Sammy thought for a second. "Cupcakes."

"Cupcakes?"

"Sure, why not? They're good, you enjoy making them, and they sell like hotcakes as soon as we put them out."

My lips twitched with a smile. "Or I could just make hotcakes?"

Sammy rolled her eyes and fought back a giggle. "What are hotcakes, anyway?"

"Pancakes." I turned around and caught the eye of Jessica, the elementary school teacher. I gestured to her that Sammy and I were going back to the kitchen and for her to keep an eye on the front.

"We should sell pancakes!"

I looked at her out of the corner of my eye. "If you can talk somebody into opening with you and helping out while you stand over a hot grill all morning, you're welcome to add it to the menu." I was far from an early bird, so I relied on Sammy to open the café each morning. She liked leaving early in the afternoon and enjoyed her morning regulars, so she didn't mind it.

"I just might do that!" She grinned at me.

We went into the kitchen behind the main part of the café, and I started gathering ingredients. "What kind?"

Sammy already had her phone up, recording me. "Whatever you feel like."

"Let's go with a classic vanilla to start. Then I don't have to worry too much yet about the kind of filling and icing."

"How do you decide that?"

"Today, it's going to be whatever ingredients speak to me."

Sammy proceeded to record the entire process of baking the cupcakes, asking nearly constant questions. It was the most bizarre baking experience I'd ever had, her phone in my face, her questioning my every move. Little did I know that it would only get weirder.

Chapter 2

"IT WAS JUST SO WEIRD. Don't you think so?" I paused in my diatribe to give my boyfriend, Matt Cardosi, aka Matteo, aka Matty, a chance to respond, but there was only silence from the living room, where Matt was sitting on the couch, catching up on some work, and—I thought—listening to me talk while I made dinner in the kitchen. "Don't you think?" I repeated myself, a little more loudly. "Matt?" Still nothing. I poked my head around the corner. "Matt!"

He jumped and slammed his laptop shut, making my dog Latte, who was sitting beside him, lift his head in confusion. "Geez, Franny, sneak up on me, why don't you?"

"You haven't been listening to me at all, have you?"

Briefly, he looked like a deer caught in the headlights. "Of course I was. I just got focused on what I was doing for a second. What were you saying again?"

"I was asking if you thought Sammy was acting weird."

His face was blank.

I pulled out the most ridiculous, un-Sammy-like thing I could come up with. "Shaving her head? Dying it pink? It's weird, isn't it?"

Matt looked appropriately shocked. "Sammy shaved her head? And dyed it pink?" He didn't seem to realize it was not remotely what I'd said before. "Is she okay? Is she going through something? I saw Ryan yesterday—" It was then that he saw the disappointed look on my face. "That's not what you were talking about, is it?"

I shook my head slowly.

"I wasn't paying attention."

"I noticed."

"I'm sorry."

I swatted him with the dish towel that lay over my shoulder. "You better be." I turned to go back in the kitchen. "Get your work in now, but you better pay attention to me over dinner."

I went over to the stove to check the temperature of the cast-iron skillet I'd been preheating. I hovered my hand a couple of inches over the surface and decided it needed a few more minutes before it was ready for the chicken breasts I planned to sear. I'd already pounded them thin and seasoned them with salt and pepper, so all they needed was a hot pan to be dropped into.

I turned to the head of romaine I had pulled out for salads and started chopping. Was Sammy's sudden obsession with videoing me in the café weird, or was I just not used to the social media era? I wasn't *that* old, but I wasn't that young either. Sammy was still in her twenties, while I was well into my thirties. Was that a big enough age gap for us to have vastly different comfort levels with social media? I didn't *feel* like a dinosaur compared to her, but maybe I was. I stopped my chopping as I realized that if my attitudes were "old" compared to Sammy's, how far behind the times must I seem to Becky, Amanda, Chloe, and Daria? I actually shuddered at the thought.

I dumped the chopped romaine into the salad spinner, rinsed it, and spun. While it drained, I started cutting tomatoes and tried not to think about being old. And then I realized I was excited about making a nice salad for dinner. That didn't mean I was getting old, did it? Being excited about salad for dinner? Salads were good! They were tasty! Sure, they weren't the fast-food burritos and milkshake coffees that the teenagers I knew seemed to live on, but liking fresh, healthy food just made me health conscious. Or so I chose to believe, at least.

I checked the heat on the skillet again. It was perfect. I drizzled some olive oil into the pan, gave it a few seconds to heat up, then gently added the chicken breasts. They started to sizzle immediately.

"Matt! Ten minutes!" I waited a beat for a response to make sure he'd heard me. Usually, I got at least a grunt in reply. "Ten minutes until dinner!" I checked the chicken breasts to make sure I liked the way they were progressing then went and stuck my head into the living room again. "Matt!"

He jumped and slammed his computer shut again. This time, Latte only opened her eyes and closed them again immediately.

"Why do you keep doing that?"

"I'm sorry, was I ignoring you again?"

"Yes, but that's not what I was talking about.

You keep closing your computer when I come around the corner like you're hiding something."

Was that a flicker of guilt that crossed his face? "Do I?"

I nodded.

"I'm not hiding anything. You just startled me. It must be a habit from work. Sometimes, I work on confidential stuff that people aren't supposed to see. That's probably all it is."

He was not a good liar. To his credit, he didn't lie often, so he didn't get much practice, but that didn't change the fact that he was obviously lying.

I thought about calling him on it but decided to let it go. If he was lying about something, it had to be for a reason. I trusted him. Didn't I?

I tried not to dwell on it as I finished putting together our salads. On top of the romaine, I added the sliced tomatoes, some extremely thin slices of mozzarella, slivers of basil from my plant out back, and some croutons I'd made by toasting the leftover garlic bread from our dinner the night before. After the chicken was cooked, I'd slice it and arrange it over the salad then add a thin drizzle of olive oil and the balsamic vinegar I'd been reducing on the stove. It was a take on a caprese salad that I found lighter yet more filling and more of an actual meal.

Besides, after the time I tried to serve a traditional one to Matt, I'd learned that his taste tended to be more for meat and potatoes than his Italian name would lead one to believe. I chalked it up to the fact that his mother had died when he was young and his dad's meal-preparation skills were stronger in the drive-through area than the healthy-home-cooking area.

My chicken breasts were beautifully browned on the skillet side, so I flipped them over to finish cooking on the other side. I dipped a spoon in the balsamic reduction. It came out coated in a thick gloss of vinegar, so I cut the heat off. It would cool just enough in the time it took me to finish dinner.

When the chicken was ready, I moved it out of the pan and onto a cutting board to rest for a few minutes while I set the table. I poured us each a glass of wine—a red, chosen because I thought it would hold up better against the sweetness of the balsamic. After everything else was done, I sliced the chicken—against the grain for the tenderest bite —and arranged it on top of the salad. I drizzled the balsamic reduction over each plate and took them to the table. "Dinner's ready!"

I pulled my chair out to sit down and then realized that with the way the night was going, I probably needed to go get Matt's attention. "Matty." I peeked around the corner. This time, he didn't slam his laptop closed, but only because he wasn't using it. He did drop his cell phone in his lap. I raised an eyebrow but didn't say anything. "Dinner's on the table."

"Oh! Okay! Great!" He hopped up and followed me into the kitchen but stopped when he saw the dishes on the table. "Oh, um, I, uh—" He glanced at the clock on the wall and then the watch on his wrist. "I was hoping we could eat on the couch."

I looked at him for a couple of seconds then at the salads on the table, each one topped with chicken that was coated in deep, dark, thick, sticky balsamic vinegar. "I'm not sure this is a good meal to eat on the couch."

He checked his watch again, looking nervous. Why was he so worried about the time?

"I thought we could watch—" And there it was. There was a game on TV that he didn't want to miss. He was wearing an old Red Sox jersey, so I guessed that was the game he wanted to catch. But he surprised me. "One of those baking shows you like. Isn't *Crazy Cake Championship* tonight?"

"*Competition: Cake Craze*," I corrected him. "And

yes, but—" I looked at the salads again, picturing chunks of chicken falling on the light-colored upholstery of the couch.

"Come on, Franny. I'm a big boy. I can eat my dinner on the couch without dropping it all over myself."

"It's not yourself I'm worried about." But I had already given in. I picked up my plate and silverware as Matt grinned and followed me. When I went back for the wine, I wished I'd chosen a white instead.

Still, as we settled in on the couch, I was excited to get to watch my show live. Matt wasn't really a fan, so I usually saved it to watch alone. If I could, I'd try to get it in before I went to work since I knew everyone at the café watched it, too, but if I didn't manage to, they were at least good at avoiding telling me who won or got kicked off. Usually. But tonight was the finale, and between customers and coworkers, it would be nearly impossible to avoid spoilers.

We turned the TV on just as the show started. I ate my chicken with my eyes on the screen. As usual, the challenge was insane—nothing a normal person would ever try. A three-tiered cake with a minimum of three flavors of sponge and three fillings in three hours.

"I don't know why any sane person would ever sign up to go on one of these shows with how crazy these challenges are," I said as the show went to commercial.

"Really? I bet you'd be great at it."

I looked at him skeptically. "I don't think so."

"Why not? You're a great baker!"

"Because they want you to do things no human can. *Three* tiers of cake in *three* flavors and *three* fillings in *three* hours? They're asking the bakers to do something insane for a gimmick."

He shrugged. "I still think you'd be great. You should audition for one."

"No."

He looked at me out of the corner of his eye and stuffed a slice of chicken into his mouth. "What if they asked you to?"

I rolled my eyes. "Really? How would they even find me? I work in a tiny coffee shop in a virtually unknown tourist town in a place no one thinks of as Cape Cod, even though it is. And if they did, it's even more unlikely that they'd want me to be on the show."

"Why not? You're a great baker."

"Because I don't make stuff like that." I gestured at the TV screen, where they were showing a selection of cakes the bakers had made over the weeks of the show. They were fondant-covered beauties and, at least according to the judges, delicious. But they weren't what I baked. I made simple, classic desserts with an occasional foray into fancy piped buttercream. But that was it. I wasn't *Competition: Cake Craze* material.

Now they were showing clips of the judging of the competition, and I remembered the other reason why I would never want to go on one of those shows: the judges. Baking Network loved to use the same judges on show after show, and their particular favorite was an angry British man who utterly destroyed ninety percent of the contestants and almost never had a good word to say about the remaining ten percent. He'd reduced more than one contestant to tears. I'd noticed that they never had him even as a guest judge on the kids' versions of any of their shows—probably because even the money-hungry network executives casting them couldn't bring themselves to subject innocent children to his unhinged rants. "I don't think I could handle being judged by him."

Matt nodded absentmindedly and stabbed his salad.

"I appreciate you thinking I could do it, though." I put my head on his shoulder for a second and then raised my lips for a kiss. He gave me a little peck but seemed distracted or unhappy. I wondered if it had anything to do with how secretive he was acting about his computer. Or maybe he was just tired. He had been working a lot, after all. Tired and stressed could explain it all.

I focused my attention on the TV, where one of the bakers had just realized she hadn't made enough cake batter to fill all her tins and was fighting off tears. I might never go on a baking competition show, but I could live vicariously through them.

"Speaking of your baking, could you make me a couple of Boston cream pies?"

I looked at him curiously.

"For work."

"Um, sure. Tomorrow okay?"

"Yeah. Tomorrow's perfect." Matt leaned forward to take a sip of wine from his glass on the coffee table. "Maybe you could have Sammy film it?"

Had he been listening earlier after all? Or did

he just think it was a good idea? Had he seen one of the videos posted? Was that why he was hiding his computer? But why would he hide a video *of* me *from* me? I was so distracted that I almost missed my fork when I reached for it. Almost. It would have been better if I'd missed it entirely. Because instead, I caught the fork against my knuckles and knocked it into a particularly balsamic-coated piece of chicken that flew out of my salad and landed on the arm of the couch next to Matt. Latte, opportunistic little creature that he was, snapped it up immediately, but the blackish stain remained.

Matt looked at me with a wry smile. "And you were worried about me getting food on the couch?"

Chapter 3

"TELL me what you're doing, Fran!" Sammy's voice was a little too loud, a little too high-pitched, and a little too stilted, like she was reading from a script.

"I'm making a Boston cream pie." My voice, in turn, was quieter and markedly lacking in the enthusiasm hers had oozed.

"Fran, come on," she said in her regular voice as she looked at me from over the phone. "Show a little excitement."

"It's just a cake."

"It's a cake?" She was back to the fake, script-reading voice. "But I thought it was a pie!"

I decided to play along, if only to get her to stop recording my every move. "I can see why you'd think that. The 'pie' in the name is actually a reference to the kind of tin it's baked in. And the fact that we didn't used to be so picky about our words for different desserts." I gave the camera a beaming smile.

Sammy grinned at me, first with a thumbs-up and then with a motion to keep going.

"It, uh—" I searched my brain for what I remembered about the origins of the pie-cake. I knew the recipe by heart—it was a simple combination of cake, custard, and ganache—but I didn't think a recipe recitation was the kind of social media content Sammy was looking for. "It was created at a famous hotel up in Boston back in the 1800s, and now it's the state dessert of Massachusetts! It's a really simple dessert but also really delicious. I think that's why it's had such staying power. It also has a really nice flavor base if you want to mix it up and add fruit or a praline to it. In fact, if I'm not mistaken, the original had almonds…"

I was on a roll now, in my element. I made the cake batter and talked about the chemistry of the sponge and the elements that made it rise versus those that other cakes used. While the cakes baked, I made the custard and talked about custards. While I gently heated the cream and chopped bars of chocolate for the ganache, I talked about the crystalline structure of tempered chocolate and how the hot cream would alter that structure and give it a pourable consistency. As the ganache cooled and firmed up on top of the cake, it would gain a glossy finish that would make the cake look extra delicious and inviting.

"So, now we just have to let everything cool, and then we'll be back with the assembly of the cake!"

Sammy blinked at me for a second before speaking. "Did you just say 'we'll be back' without me prompting you?"

I smiled awkwardly. "I think I did."

"Aww, you're getting used to this." She came over and gave me a one-armed hug. With the other arm, she held out her phone to take a selfie. "That one is going on our socials for real!"

"For real? Is all the rest of this pretend?"

She looked startled. "What? No! Of course it's all real. It's all really going on our socials, I mean. It'll take a few days to edit together and all, so you won't see it there yet, but it's all definitely real." Her pale cheeks flushed as she rushed her words out.

"Are you okay?"

"Yes, of course. Just thinking about how we

need to edit all of this together. I guess I could have gone live with it, but I didn't think about it. So now I have to—"

She turned and walked back out into the front part of the café without finishing her sentence. She seemed distracted and a little overwhelmed. I wondered if she needed some time off.

A little while later, after the cakes and custard were cool, we'd both eaten, the lunchtime rush was over, and Sammy came back from the break she'd tried to convince me she didn't need, we reconvened to finish the cakes.

It took me a few minutes to warm up to the camera in my face again, but soon enough, I was chattering away like I was on my own cooking show. If I'd stopped to think about it, I would have felt ridiculous, but every time I even paused, Sammy motioned for me to keep going, and so I did, and I somehow managed to talk my way through the whole assembly of the cakes. As I finished, I held one up and tilted it ever so slightly toward the camera. "And so, you see, it's a simple cake but simply delicious." I paused for a second. "That was stupid. Let me try it again."

"No, it was perfect!" Sammy's eye twinkled.

"We could make it a weekly feature and call it Simply Delicious."

For a moment, thoughts of internet fame swirled in my head. I could be on TV. I could have my own TV show! It would be great for the café—we'd get so much business. I could expand, hire even more people. And then I remembered that I would have to bake with a camera in my face the whole time, and my bubble burst.

"Nope. I enjoy baking it. I'm not going to ruin that by adding a camera to record my every move. It makes me too self-conscious about what I'm doing." I stopped and thought a second. "Actually, I don't remember if I even stopped to taste anything along the way." I looked at Sammy to see if she'd noticed.

She shrugged and then smiled. "It would be wrong to serve something to people that we hadn't taste tested."

I smiled, too, as I saw where her mind was going. I'd made four cakes—two for Matt and two to sell by the slice in the café. "You're right. It would be." I picked up the long cake knife that could slice all the way across a cake in one cut. "We'll just have to try the first slice ourselves."

"I'm willing to make that sacrifice for our

customers." She attempted a solemn look but broke into a smile halfway through.

"Grab a plate," I told her as I eyed the cake, knife in hand. I had gained a lot of confidence about slicing cakes in the past year that I'd been working in the café full-time, but that first cut always triggered a brief wave of anxiety. It was even worse in a ganache-coated cake like this one. Any false cut marks would be visible. I had only one shot to make perfect slices.

I lined the knife up as best I could and lowered it into the cake. There was the slightest bit of resistance as I cut through the ganache layer, but then the knife glided through the remaining layers of cake and custard with ease. Perfect. I wiped the knife off and lowered it into the cake again. The wiping was a key step that ensured neat slices. If you didn't wipe the knife in between cuts, you'd get bits of cake and icing built up on it, and your slices wouldn't be clean and perfect. I repeated my motions, wiping and slicing, until I had twelve perfect—or almost perfect—slices. Then I carefully removed it and put it on the plate Sammy had brought over. We picked up our forks, and I nodded at her to go first.

"Oh, no. Chef first."

I shrugged and used my fork to cut off a bite. A smile crossed my face as soon as it touched my tongue. I nodded happily at Sammy. She dug straight in for her own first bite. Neither of us spoke as we polished off the piece of cake. It was heavenly. And no wonder it had been popular for one hundred fifty years. Between the chocolatey glaze, the creamy custard, and the buttery cake, it was perfection.

"We'd better get this out front before we eat it all." Sammy was joking, but there was just enough truth to it that I nodded and pushed the cake plate toward her. I could easily—and happily—polish off another slice, but if we liked it that much, customers would too.

"Take this one out. We'll keep the second one back here until that one's gone. If any of the girls want to try a piece, they're welcome to."

Sammy took the cake out front while I sliced and put the second one away then boxed up Matt's two cakes. I shot him a quick text to let him know they were ready.

He replied almost immediately. *You're the best! Love you!* Followed by a kissy-face emoji. I smiled and sent the same emoji back.

I should have known better than to think I had

anything to worry about with him. He had probably just been tired and stressed last night.

Then I got another text from him. *Pies are ready! Can I meet you in the morning to give them to you?*

I stared at the message until my screen started to dim. I sent back a question mark.

It was a long few seconds before Matt's response came in. *Sorry, that was for Mindy. She's in charge of the party.*

I knew Mindy. Mindy was his office's administrative assistant. It made sense that she was the one responsible for organizing the food for the party. But something still felt wrong about it.

I was still staring at my phone—now with a dark screen—when Sammy stuck her head in the back. "The girls want to know if you want to go get Mexican with them tonight. They're calling it a team-building event."

"We'll have to wait forever to get a table." It was mid–tourist season, and every sit-down restaurant had a line out the door as hungry families tried to find something to eat that didn't involve standing over a hot stove after a long day in the sun.

"Rhonda already called and got us on the list. Table will be ready in an hour."

Of course, there was that option too. Several of

the restaurants in town—the ones that were open during the off-season and had managed to stay in business for more than a year or two—had a secret call-ahead list. There wasn't a password or anything sneaky like that, but if you were a regular and mentioned that when you called, you could get on the wait list and show up close to your seating time instead of waiting outside in line for hours. The unspoken rule was that you couldn't make it obvious that was what you were doing. Don't show up immediately before your table was ready and don't loudly announce that you had called ahead. Either of those things would be sure to cancel your call-ahead privileges.

I looked at my phone for a few more seconds and then nodded. It would be good to go out with the girls for a night.

Chapter 4

I TRIED to engage with the banter around the table, but my heart wasn't in it. I kept catching myself staring out the window and thinking about Matt. He'd been acting so strange the past couple of days. I didn't understand it.

Rhonda leaned over and whispered, "Are you okay?"

I nodded. "Just have some things on my mind."

"Anything you want to talk about?"

I hesitated and looked around the table. Rhonda and I were at the far end. Everyone else was engaged in a lively conversation about a reality show I didn't watch but was apparently all the rage.

"Anything you say is between you and me. You know that."

I nodded but looked around the table again. I didn't exactly want to air my relationship woes at a table filled with my young employees, even if it seemed like they weren't listening.

"We could go for a walk after?" Rhonda was determined to give me a chance to open up.

"Yeah, maybe," I agreed reluctantly.

Rhonda nodded with a sympathetic look on her face and patted my hand.

"You watch it, don't you, Miss Fran?"

I turned and looked down the table. Chloe was looking at me expectantly. I had no idea what she was asking if I watched, but I did know one thing. "You don't have to call me 'Miss Fran.' Just Fran is fine." She looked so uneasy with the request that I rushed to change it. "But you don't have to. Whatever you're comfortable with is fine. But what show were you asking about?"

"Competition: Cake Craze. You watch it, don't you?" Chloe looked nervous, as if I would bite her head off for speaking to me.

I smiled as warmly as I could, wanting to soothe her nerves. "I do! Did you all catch the finale last night?"

That set off a whirlwind of chatter. They'd all watched it, and they were all excited to discuss the surprise win of the stay-at-home mom from Maine.

"She's a wicked-good baker," Daria said. "And fierce. The way she stood up to the judge when he called her flavors cliché? That was goals."

"Total goals," Chloe said.

"I really respect her determination," Becky said as Amanda nodded beside her. "Nothing he said got under her skin. Ever."

Rhonda and I exchanged a smile at the different ways the girls expressed themselves. There was only a couple of years' age difference between them—Chloe and Daria had just finished their freshman year of high school, while Becky and Amanda were going to be seniors—but those couple years made a big difference in them. There were times when Chloe and Daria still looked like kids—awkward and unsure of themselves but trying to act like grown-ups. More often than not, Becky and Amanda had started looking like young women. And working around the younger girls in the café seemed to be reinforcing that—I noticed them trying harder to be responsible and proactive in their work, even stepping in to help train Chloe and Daria. I was proud of them.

"The male judge on that show gets under my

skin," said Jessica, the elementary school teacher. "What's his name? Jeremy Johnson?" Several of us nodded. "He's so condescending. Positive reinforcement is so much better for growth and learning than negative. I wish he'd learn that."

"I don't think he wants them to get better," Donna said. She was Rhonda's friend and the last new member of our staff. I knew her the least, but I liked what I saw so far. "If they got better, they might end up being better than him. He just wants to be an—" She cut herself off and glanced around at the teenagers at the table with us. "A jerk because he thinks it makes him look big and powerful next to them. But men like that, let me tell you, men like that are small. They are small, and you girls should never let yourselves fall for that kind of man's nonsense. You're better than that and better than him." She looked each girl in the eye, even Chloe, who was reluctant to make eye contact. Then Donna looked at me and seemed to realize that it was not necessarily a good thing to go off on an opinionated tirade in front of your new boss.

Fortunately, I agreed with every word out of her mouth and gave her an approving smile.

She smiled back and looked at each of the girls again. "And if you girls ever aren't sure if a man is cutting you down or building you up, you come to one of us ladies, because you know we'll always have your back."

"Hear! Hear!" I lifted my water glass and held it toward the middle of the table. Rhonda, Donna, Jessica, and Sammy all immediately picked up their glasses to toast. The younger girls took a little longer to figure it out but eventually lifted their glasses and clinked them against ours.

The food came right after our toast, so a few minutes went by quietly as we all settled into our meals. Then Sammy spoke up. "Have you ever thought about going on one of those shows, Fran?"

I had just taken a bite of my taco, so I had to chew and swallow before I could answer. "Not really. Matt keeps mentioning it, but I don't think it would be for me."

"Why not?" Daria asked.

"Partly, I'm busy here with the café. And a lot of the people on those shows are professional pastry chefs—I don't think my skills are quite on their level." I suddenly felt awkward about my reasons with all of them looking at me. "And Jeremy Johnson judges half of those shows. I don't want to deal with him."

"Don't let a small man like that hold you down,

Fran." Amanda's voice came from the other end of the table.

I looked at her in shock. She was one of the quietest people I'd ever met, rarely speaking up except when taking customers' orders or when she was asked a direct question. She was kind and sweet but beyond the normal bounds of quiet. To hear her now was surprising. And, honestly, it made my excuses sound even weaker.

"You know, you're right, Amanda. I shouldn't let Jeremy Johnson's negativity put me off going on a baking show. I still don't think I'll be applying for one, but I won't let him be one of the reasons I don't." I smiled at them and hoped that would be the end of it. I should have known better.

"Gloria Harris is a stay-at-home mom, and she just won," Becky said.

"You're an amazing baker. My mom is always asking me to bring home leftovers," Chloe added.

"We sold out of the Boston cream pie in half an hour," Daria said.

"My boys can't get enough of your cookies," Rhonda said. "I don't even bother making them myself anymore because they like yours so much."

"Really?" I asked, looking at Rhonda. "You're getting in on this too?"

She shrugged and grinned. "Well, they're right."

I sighed. "All right, all right, I'll think about it. Does that make you all happy?"

The adult women nodded, but the teenagers looked at each other for confirmation first. It was as if they didn't want to call a cease-fire unless all parties agreed. Finally, they did.

"Can we finish our dinners now?" I took another bite to drive the suggestion home. When they did, too, I figured I was in the clear. At least for now. I could only hope they didn't bring it up again or conspire among themselves to apply on my behalf. I really didn't want to go on TV.

Chapter 5

RHONDA LINGERED near me as we all said our goodbyes after dinner. "You want to take that walk?" she asked quietly.

I was about to say no, but then I remembered how weird Matt had been acting and nodded.

Rhonda inclined her head toward the beach, and I nodded again. We finished saying goodbye to the other girls, waiting until they had all gone so no one tried to join us for a moonlight beach stroll, and then crossed the parking lot and headed down to the beach.

We slipped our shoes off and carried them as we started along the sand. It was counterintuitive to a lot of people who weren't from the area, but on this part of the coastline, the shore ran almost east–

west instead of north–south. We headed east, back toward Main Street and the café. I stared toward the water. There was still a faint light in the sky behind us, but in front of us, the sky was black. It felt disturbingly like a reflection of my life.

"So, what's going on?" Rhonda asked after a few minutes.

I stared out at the water for a few more steps. It seemed impossible to say it out loud, but I knew I needed another perspective. Rhonda had the bluntness of a true Bay Stater, but she was also fair and levelheaded. I trusted her to tell me like it was and not sugarcoat things.

"I think Matt is cheating on me." I blurted it out without looking at her, only glancing her way out of the corner of my eye for a brief second.

"What?" She stopped in her tracks, her shout loud enough that a group of people having a bonfire farther up the beach turned to look our way. "You think Matt is *cheating* on you?" She took a second to attempt to compose herself. "Why? What's going on?"

I stopped a few feet in front of her and turned to face the water. "He's been acting—I don't know —weird. And distant." I looked over at her to see what she was making of my vague description then back out at the water. "He slams his computer shut or puts down his phone every time I walk into the room."

"Sounds like my boys," Rhonda muttered, rolling her eyes. "It's different with a grown man, of course. At least, you'd hope."

"He asked me to make him two Boston cream pies."

"Is that a euphemism for something?"

"He said they were for a party at work, but after I texted him that they were ready, he accidentally texted me, asking if he could meet me in the morning to give me the pies. He said he meant to send it to the admin at work because she was organizing the party, but why wouldn't he just take them to her? And why would he text her about it?"

Rhonda's eyes met mine with compassion. She walked over and put her hand on my shoulder. "I think it's going to be okay. I really do."

"Something's going on, Rhonda." My throat started to get tight. "I just know it. He's not acting like himself."

"Maybe it's something to do with work. Is he working on any new projects?"

I blinked back the tears that were filling my eyes. "I don't think so. He hasn't told me. He suggested watching *Competition: Cake Craze* last night. He doesn't even like that show."

Something flickered across Rhonda's face. She'd heard my lighthearted complaints about Matt not wanting to watch it in the past, so she understood what a big deal it was that he had volunteered to watch it.

"See? I told you it was bad."

She put her hands on my shoulders and turned me to face her. "Franny, listen to me. You know I call it like I see it, and I don't tiptoe around people's feelings when they need to hear the truth."

I nodded, bracing myself for her to tell me that I was right, that Matt was cheating, that I had to break up with him and move on with my life before it was too late and I tethered myself to a man who was going to make me miserable.

"Matt is not cheating on you. Everything is fine. He's just trying to be a good boyfriend. I promise you, everything will be fine."

I wanted to believe her, really, I did, but Matt's behavior had just been too strange, too unusual. I went home that night feeling sick to my stomach about it all.

I swung by the café for the two Boston cream pies I'd set aside for Matt. I tried to tuck the cake boxes under my arm, but they were an awkward fit. One probably would have been okay, but two just made it uncomfortable. I shifted them around, trying to find the best way to carry both of them, but nothing felt right, so I ended up parading through the streets with them in front of me. A carful of teenagers drove slowly past me, making me feel all the more uncomfortable. I just wanted to be home, curled up in my cozy Cape Cod–style house with my dog and my boyfriend who wasn't acting weird at all. Under the circumstances, I decided that it would be enough to curl up on the couch with them and just pretend everything was normal.

As I rounded the corner onto my street, I was surprised to see the lights on in Matt's house and, two houses down, the lights off in my own. Usually, he helped me out and went by my place to let Latte out and ended up staying there to wait for me. We didn't officially live together—I was cautious about making that leap without a commitment, especially when we lived so close to each other—but we did spend virtually every evening together and spent the night more often than not. The few times we didn't were when one of us had to get up early and didn't want to disturb the other.

I decided that Matt must have taken Latte back to his place, which was something he did on occasion, and went and knocked on his door. There was no telltale barking to indicate Latte's presence, but he wasn't always the best of guard dogs. I jokingly attributed his laissez-faire attitude to the French origins of his breed. The genetic testing I'd had done on him had showed that he was a purebred Berger Picard, but when I'd found him, he was a stray.

Matt looked briefly surprised to see me when he answered the door, but then a big smile spread across his face. "Hey, gorgeous. Pies delivered right to my door, huh? Perks of dating the baker!" He leaned in to take the cake boxes from me and brushed a kiss across my lips. "Come on in."

I looked around as I stepped inside but didn't see Latte anywhere. "Is Latte here?"

"Oh, uh, no. I just got home. A few minutes ago. I haven't been down to take him out yet."

I felt bad for my poor pup. "I'd better get down to the house and let him out, then." I circled back toward the door. Matt had put the cakes in the fridge and looked as if he was heading for the couch with a glass of neat bourbon. "You coming?"

"Oh, yeah, of course." He stopped midsit, put

the bourbon on the end table, and moved to follow me to the door.

"Your drink?"

"I'll get it later."

It seemed like a weird choice to me, but I wasn't a straight-liquor drinker, so I didn't know if it was unusual to leave it sitting out overnight like that. I just shrugged and headed for the door.

Matt followed me out the door, not bothering to lock it behind him. I'd grown up in Cape Bay and been back in town for more than a year, but my years living and working in New York City had gotten me into the habit of locking my house and car every time I went into or out of them. Sometimes, it seemed as if I was the only person in town who followed that basic safety procedure, though.

We walked down to follow the sidewalk to my house instead of crossing our neighbor's yard like we used to do when we were kids. The people who had lived in the house then were a friendly older couple who liked watching us run around, but there were new people there now, and we weren't cute little kids anymore. Well, I thought Matt was still pretty cute, but I didn't think the neighbors agreed.

I didn't hear a peep from Latte until we were inside and I called up the stairs. There was a pause then a doggie yawn before he finally came trotting down the stairs to greet us with some sniffs. As usual, he was particularly thorough about my work clothes. Matt only got a cursory sniff, as he'd already changed into basketball shorts and a Red Sox shirt that had seen better days.

I fed Latte and let him out then stood on the back patio with Matt while he and Latte played fetch. I felt my worries about Matt's behavior melting away as they played and Matt and I chatted about our days. Everything was fine. I had just been imagining things thinking Matt's behavior was suspicious.

Latte eventually got tired and lay down with his ball at Matt's feet instead of dropping it and running back out into the yard. He rolled onto his side and lay there, panting, with his tongue lolling out.

"Looks like I wore him out." Matt chuckled softly.

The sound of his low laugh triggered a warm, pleasant tightness in my stomach. I took his hand and leaned in to kiss him. "I'm pretty worn out too. Maybe we should make it an early night."

Matt smiled and bent his head, covering my lips with his.

I reached up and wound my fingers in his hair.

His phone blinged, and he reached into his pocket and pulled it out. He looked at it for a few seconds then dropped it back into his pocket.

But instead of getting back to kissing me or taking me by the hand and leading me inside, he brushed his thumb against my lower lip with a slight smile. "I guess I better head home and let you get to bed."

I took a step back to look at him better. Did he not understand why I was suggesting an early bedtime? Were my not-so-subtle hints too subtle? "You're not going to stay here tonight?"

"Nah, I've got an early morning."

I stepped forward again and wrapped my arms around his waist. "That's okay. You know I'm a heavy sleeper."

"The pies are at my house. I have to give them to Mindy first thing in the morning."

Was it just my imagination, or had there been a slight hesitation in his voice before he said Mindy's name? "You can get them in the morning." Something flickered across his face. "Is everything okay, Matty?"

He smiled down at me, tipping my chin up with his forefinger. "Of course, Franny." He kissed me softly. "I'll see you tomorrow." He squeezed my hand, bent down to scratch Latte's head, and then strode off across the neighbor's backyard to his own house, leaving me staring after him. He looked back and waved before disappearing inside.

I stood on the patio, looking toward his house, for several long minutes until Latte got my attention by nudging my hand with his nose. I looked down into his big, innocent eyes. They looked sympathetic.

With a last glance toward Matt's house, I opened the back door. Latte and I settled down on the couch and cuddled, with Baking Network playing mindlessly on the TV screen. The last thing I remembered was a commercial for an upcoming new show called *Hometown Showdown*, with Jeremy Johnson as one of the judges. I pitied the poor people with the bad luck to end up on that show.

Chapter 6

THE NEXT MORNING and well into the afternoon, the café was so busy I didn't even have time to think, which I was grateful for, because every time I had a moment to breathe, my mind immediately went to Matt and how strange he'd been acting. I even put Sammy in charge of the midday cookie baking so I could distract myself with customers—it was too easy to let my mind wander when I was mixing and stirring and scooping out dough. Usually, it was one of my favorite aspects of the process, but not today—not when I needed to keep my mind occupied.

I left the counter in Chloe's and Jessica's hands and made my way around the café's tables to top off coffees and clear dirty dishes. I chatted with a few people I knew, either from growing up or because they were regulars, and I smiled pleasantly at everyone I didn't.

"You're Fran, right?" one woman asked as I refilled her coffee cup. I didn't recognize her, but her manner suggested she knew me.

"Sure am."

"I'm Gail." She said it as if it would mean something to me. It didn't.

I searched my brain for any idea who she might be and came up blank. Neither her name nor her face rang any bells.

"It's a pleasure to meet you, Gail." I let my gaze drift on to the next table. The woman there caught my eye and gave a slight motion to her coffee cup. I smiled in acknowledgment. I was about to step away when Gail stopped me.

"I'm very impressed with your baking. Did you go to culinary school?"

I turned back toward her reluctantly but tried to keep my feelings out of my voice. "Nope! I learned everything I know about baking from my grandparents and my mother."

"That's fabulous. The family connection is a great story."

I nodded and smiled, gesturing with one finger

at the next table to let the woman there know I hadn't forgotten her and was on my way.

"This was your grandparents' café, right?" She gestured around at the walls of the coffee shop.

"Sure was! They started it when they came over from Italy."

"That's great. Outstanding. People love a story like that."

I had to stop myself from looking around to see if anyone had overheard and if they thought it was as weird a comment as I did. I was ready to extricate myself from the situation however I could. "Okay, well, I better—"

"Your Boston cream pie was delicious."

I stopped and looked at her. "Were you here yesterday?" Maybe that was why she had acted like she knew me—maybe I had spoken to her the day before. I thought I would have remembered her, though—I was pretty good with faces. But yesterday had been the first time I'd made Boston cream pie for the café in ages. Unless...

"No, this is my first time in here! It's adorable! So cozy and New England-y. Did you do the—"

"Do you work with Matt?"

Gail's face lit up. "Yes! I've been working with Matt! He's such a sweetheart, isn't he?"

I felt my stomach tie itself in knots. "Yes. He is. He's my boyfriend, you know." I couldn't keep the harsh edge out of my voice.

"Oh, yes, of course! He speaks so highly of you! And your baking."

She winked at me—actually winked!

"I need to get back to work," I said, a good bit more curtly than I would ever speak to a customer under normal circumstances.

"You have great screen presence. The way you talk about your baking really shows your passion. You come across as very warm and relatable."

Everything Gail said felt oddly personal, almost as if she was needling me, trying to get under my skin—talking to me as if she knew me, gushing over Matt, bringing up the social media videos Sammy had made that I hadn't even realized she'd posted already. Who was this woman, and what did she want from me? Why was she saying these things? And why did I have a nagging feeling that she had something to do with Matt's weird behavior lately?

But no. She couldn't. That was crazy. That was stress talking and finding connections where there weren't any.

I realized she was still looking at me, waiting for

me to respond to her compliment about my so-called "screen presence."

"Thank you. That's very kind of you."

"You're a great personality."

"Thank you." I gritted my teeth as Chloe walked around the counter, carrying a coffee pot, and went straight for the table next to me. It was great that she was taking initiative and helping out with refills when she saw me get waylaid by a customer, but her stepping up took away my excuse to move on from Gail.

I glanced around frantically—and as discreetly as I could—looking for someone, anyone, who could give me an excuse to walk away. I even briefly found myself hoping that Sammy would burn a batch of cookies and set off the fire alarm so we would have to evacuate the café—although, to be honest, I wouldn't actually evacuate. I would run to put out the fire. Even an imaginary café fire was terrifying. Antonia's was the legacy of three generations of my family's life and work. I shook the thought of a fire out of my head.

Gail was still talking. "I think you'll be—"

I almost jumped out of my skin with excitement when the café door opened and I saw Mrs. D'Angelo walk in. Normally, she drove me crazy with the way she literally held me captive with her long red fingernails when she was talking to me and never let me get a word in edgewise, but today, I was thrilled. "If you'll excuse me, I have to go speak to some-one." I smiled graciously at Gail before hurrying off in the direction of Mrs. D'Angelo. "Mrs. D'Angelo! How are you?"

Mrs. D'Angelo immediately sank her talons into my upper arm, grasping me as though I wanted to get away. "Francesca! I'm so glad you're working today! I need to talk to you about an order for the Ladies' Auxiliary. Now, I know you're very busy, but…"

BY THE END of the day, I was exhausted. We'd stayed busy into the evening, and I'd had to keep Sammy late so she could work on the cookies Mrs. D'Angelo just *had* to have for her Ladies' Auxiliary meeting, which was, of course, that night. As I locked up the café, I rubbed the spot on my arm where I was pretty sure I could see the marks from Mrs. D'Angelo's claws—uh, fingernails.

My phone rang as I started down Main Street toward my house. I pulled it out of my bag and smiled when I saw that it was Matt. A split second later, I remembered how I felt he'd been acting strange lately. I'd been so busy all day that I'd actually managed to forget.

"Hi, honey. I just locked up the café. I'm exhausted," I said by way of answering.

Matt laughed in that low chuckle I liked so much. "So I guess you won't argue about a quiet night in?"

"Actually, I was thinking we could go grab something. I don't even want to think about having to cook."

"We could order in."

I thought for a moment, trying to come up with something that both sounded good and was available to have delivered. I came up with nothing. "I want something other than pizza. Let's just go out."

There was a pause for a moment, and I assumed Matt was trying to think of where we could go eat. I was too tired to think. Before he even said anything, I knew I would agree to whatever he suggested. "There's, uh, a game I want to watch tonight. I'll miss the start of it if we go out."

Except that. My only option was to pitch Matt's favorite sports bar. "We could go over to Duffy's." He never turned down Duffy's. "I'm sure they'll have whatever game it is on, and if they don't, you can ask. I'm sure they can put it on one of their ninety TVs."

"It's seventy-five."

"Whatever. I'm sure they'll have your game." I was mentally plotting out the salad I would order. For a sports bar, they had surprisingly delicious salads. Was I really getting excited about having salad for dinner *again*?

"Wait, did I say game? It's not a game. It's a—" There was a definite pause. "A game *show*. One of those ninja-warrior obstacle course things."

"I'm sure they would be happy to put that on for you."

"They wouldn't," he said a little too quickly. The tension in my stomach was returning. "They, uh, they have a policy against it."

"They have a *policy* against obstacle course shows?" I repeated incredulously.

"Yeah, uh, I think a fight broke out one time when they let someone put one on."

"A *fight* broke out over an obstacle course show? A fistfight? Are you messing with me?"

"No, I'm not! I think the guy was mad that they were showing that instead of a football game, but, you know, anyway, they're banned now."

If I had been hearing this from anyone but Matt, it would sound like an elaborate lie. A completely ridiculous, elaborate lie. But Matt didn't lie to me. Did he? "Okay, um, well..." I tried to think of another place I could suggest. I just wanted to go out and grab a quick bite to eat before collapsing on the couch and staring mindlessly at the TV, even if what was on was some oversized-kids' game.

"I could go to Sandy's Seafood Shack and get us a couple of burgers and fries."

"Okay, fine," I said quickly. I was too tired to argue about it anymore. I just wanted to sit down and have food put in front of me. If it had to be Matt putting a burger in front of me, that was fine.

"Great! I'll go now so we can eat before—before the show starts."

"Um, okay." I was close enough to the house that I could have asked him to wait two minutes until I got there, but I was tired of trying to figure out his weird thought process tonight—or during the past few days, for that matter. "I'll be at my place."

"Actually, can you come down to my house?"

I sighed. "Okay, whatever."

"I'll be back in twenty minutes."

"Don't forget to call ahead so you don't have to wait in line forever."

"Will do. See you soon."

"I love you," I said.

Silence.

I looked at the phone and realized he'd already hung up.

A deep sadness came over me. Something was definitely wrong.

Chapter 7

I WENT HOME to get changed out of my coffee-stained work clothes and feed Latte before heading over to Matt's. Matt obviously hadn't been over to let Latte out again. Since I was just going to eat takeout at Matt's, I pulled on an old, paint-stained T-shirt and a pair of sweatpants that had seen better days. I pulled my thick mass of black hair out of the chignon I kept it in for work and raked it into a messy bun on the top of my head.

I told myself I'd wash my face later but knew that was more than a little bit unlikely. Terrible for my skin but unlikely. I tried to rub away the black mascara circles that had formed under my eyes when I'd stood over the steamy sink, washing the last of the day's dishes, but wasn't very successful. I told myself that I looked fine and Matt wouldn't care. He loved me no matter how I looked. At least, I thought he did.

I didn't even bother putting Latte on a leash to walk out my back door (locking it behind me, of course) and over to Matt's. He trotted politely beside me. The one time he did start to veer off to sniff a bunny trail, I patted my leg, and he came running right back. At least *he* wasn't acting strangely at all.

We went in through Matt's unlocked back door. I grabbed a bottle of red wine, a corkscrew, and two glasses and headed through to the living room. Matt's house and mine were exactly the same except mirror images of each other. And the décor, of course. Matt's house had suffered from thirtyish years of steady bachelor occupation—first, when he and his dad had lived there after his mom died and then when Matt lived there alone after his dad's passing—and it was more than evident in the ancient furniture and pictures that hadn't been updated since Matt started grade school.

I plopped down on the worn couch, opened the bottle of wine, and poured us each a generous glass. I closed my eyes briefly to savor the taste as I took a sip and realized that if Matt didn't make it back soon, I might fall asleep right there.

Latte hopped up beside me and laid his head on my knee, looking up at me with his best puppy-dog eyes.

"Sorry, boy, you wouldn't like this. And Matty won't be home with fries to sneak to you for a little while."

He sniffed like he was displeased with the wait but seemed to accept my head pat as an apology. He gave my sweatpants a lick and let his eyes slowly close. I took another sip of the wine and started to feel my own eyelids grow heavy. Matt needed to hurry.

I leaned carefully to pick up the remote, trying not to disturb Latte's position. I turned the TV on and pulled up the guide to look for Matt's show for him. While I had long since cut the cord and switched to all-streaming TV, Matt still had a high-end cable package that, as far as I could tell, included every televised sporting event anywhere in the world. I was pretty sure I had once caught him watching Bangladesh playing cricket. Really, I shouldn't have been surprised that he was so invested in watching a ninja obstacle course show. It probably wasn't even in English.

I scrolled through the channels, looking for anything that could possibly be his show. Of course, with what seemed like three thousand channels, I knew I could be scrolling for quite a while and never even find it. I paused on the Baking Network to see what was on, only to find that it was *Bake for Your Life!* (exclamation point included), one of my least favorite shows. It was too fake, too overdramatized. They put the bakers in ridiculous situations, and they had to bake well using things like literal sticks and rocks to advance to the next round. Sometimes I wondered why I watched that channel at all. Still, I didn't change it. I watched some poor girl arrange balls of cookie dough on a rock while dripping wet after climbing through a "stream" to get it. Two of the balls rolled off just as the host announced there were only fifteen minutes left in the challenge, and the show cut to commercial. There was another reason I never wanted to be on a baking show—who knew what kind of crazy thing they'd make you do?

A commercial for *Hometown Showdown* came on. It flashed famous sights and buildings from different cities around the country before cutting to Jeremy Johnson with a typically smug look on his face. "Do *you* have what it takes to win your hometown's showdown?" he asked in his overwrought upper-crust British accent. The words *Now Casting on the East Coast!* flashed up on the screen with a list of cities from Portland, Maine, to Miami, Florida. I rolled my eyes and started scrolling channels again. Putting Jeremy Johnson in a casting commercial seemed like the opposite of a good way to get people to sign up for a show. I didn't know what sane baker would willingly subject themselves to his nastiness. Signing up for a show on which he was a judge actually seemed like a prime indicator that someone was *not* sane.

Matt burst through the door as I scrolled through multiple channels of a collegiate cornhole tournament. "Have you seen this? Are cornhole players considered college athletes now?"

"It's intramural." He dumped the bags from Sandy's on the coffee table and grabbed his laptop from where it was sitting on an armchair before sitting down beside me. "Could you turn that off?"

I looked at him in confusion. "I was looking for your show."

"My what? Oh, my show. Yeah, we'll get to that. We just have to do this meeting real quick."

"A meeting? What meeting?" I turned to face him, jostling Latte. "Matt, what's going on?"

"What? Nothing. I just—we have to do this real quick. I lost track of time."

"What are you talking about? What do we have to do? I don't understand! I thought we were watching this show. I—"

"Here, scoot next to me." He angled the computer so that both our faces appeared in the frame from the webcam.

"Scoot next to you? What's going on? Why are we on camera? Could you turn it off? I—"

He moved closer to me, adjusting the angle so we were both fully on the screen. I didn't know if it was his computer or the effects of the day, but I looked terrible through the camera. I really hoped it was a camera issue.

"Smile, Franny," he said and clicked the Connect button.

It felt as if my heart stopped as Gail's face popped up on the screen. I started to get up, but Matt grabbed my arm and pulled me back down. He slid his hand into mine.

"Matt, what's going on?" My words came out as barely a whisper. I didn't know what was happening or why or how Matt knew this woman who acted like she knew me or why she was on his computer screen when we were supposed to be watching grown adults navigate an oversized-playground obstacle course.

"Hi, Gail!" Matt's voice was almost-painfully cheerful. "How are you today?"

"I'm great, Matt! How are you?"

My mind swirled as they exchanged banal pleasantries. There was clearly a reason this woman had come to my café today and insisted on talking to me. There was clearly a reason we were having this video call. I looked at Matt, but he was smiling at Gail's face on the computer. I tried to swallow but couldn't get it past the knot in my throat.

"Doin' good, doin' good. I'm sorry we're late! I ran out to pick us up some dinner, and the time just got away from me. I always forget how busy places get around here during the tourist season."

"Not a problem. I stopped by Antonia's Italian Café today, and I noticed how busy they were. It's a good sign! I hope they won't miss Fran too much!"

I had started to feel as if the world was moving in slow motion. Nothing they were saying made sense. "Why will the café miss me? Where am I going?" My voice was still hoarse and whispery.

Matt and Gail both chuckled good-naturedly and seemed to exchange a glance through the camera.

"She really has no idea, does she, Matt?"

"Not a clue! I think we've been very sneaky."

I wanted to throw up. Or cry. Or both. My thoughts flew at a million miles an hour. Matt had been acting weird because of Gail. Matt was cheating with Gail. Gail was about to ruin my life.

"Should I go ahead and tell her?" Gail looked excited.

"Let's do it." Matt looked at me with a massive grin on his face and his phone in his hand. He was recording me. He was recording the moment that my life was ruined. I fought to keep control of my stomach and my tears.

"Francesca Amaro," Gail began, a ridiculous grin on her face. "We at the Baking Network are thrilled to announce that you are going to be part of the Boston episode of *Hometown Showdown*, hosted by Jeremy Johnson!"

Chapter 8

I STARED BLANKLY at Matt's laptop screen and Gail's face on it. Was I hallucinating? That had to be it. I was hallucinating. I touched my forehead to check for a fever then pinched myself—hard. Probably too hard.

"Say something!" Matt hissed, his eyes wide and a forced smile plastered on his face. On the screen, Gail's own smile had started to look strained.

A strangled laugh forced its way out of my throat. I shook my head sharply. "I'm sorry, I—" I blinked hard. "I thought you said you want me to be on the Baking Network."

Gail's smile perked up. "That's exactly what I said! I don't know if you've seen our commercials— I think Matt said you have—but we're casting a great new show called *Hometown Showdown*, where bakers from cities across the country compete to make the absolute *best* version of their hometown desserts!"

Matt stared at me while I stared at Gail, still not believing what I was hearing. That didn't stop her, though.

"We're coming to Boston soon, and our bakers are making—what else—Boston cream pie!"

"I'm—I'm not—I'm not a baker," I stammered. "I—I own a coffee shop. I—I make coffee. That's what I do. I'm not a baker."

Matt elbowed me in the side.

Gail didn't even seem fazed. "Oh, I would disagree about that, Fran. I've had your Boston cream pie, remember? So good! Delicious!" She leaned toward the screen. "I really shouldn't be saying this, but—well, I know we haven't even gotten started yet, but after eating your pie, I think you're an early front-runner."

"A frontrunner? In what?" I knew I should know, but my brain felt as if it was slogging through mud. I understood all of the words Gail was saying and knew her sentences made sense—I just couldn't connect them.

"In the Boston episode of *Hometown Showdown*, of course!"

I blinked.

Gail did not. She turned her wide stare toward Matt. "Is she all right, Matt? I think we threw her for a loop with the announcement!" She chuckled awkwardly.

Matt echoed her laughter. "I think so!" He put his arm around me and squeezed. "Cape Bay's a small town, and I think Franny's just a little surprised that the Baking Network found her and invited her on! Right, Franny?"

I nodded, even though "surprised" didn't even begin to cover my feelings on the matter.

"Well, you have Matt to thank for that." Gail beamed. "He's the one who got in touch with us and convinced us to try your food. I have to say, I think this is the first time we've ever been able to completely surprise a baker with the invitation."

They both looked at me silently. "Thank you," I said and patted Matt's leg.

Gail chuckled awkwardly again. "Well, I'll let you two get back to your evening. I'll be in touch so we can get all the paperwork signed and make sure you have all the filming details."

I nodded silently.

"Sounds good, Gail! Thanks for all your help surprising Franny. I'm sure everything will be a lot easier to arrange now that she knows."

"Oh, I'm sure. Thank you, Matt, for facilitating everything so far, and congratulations again, Fran. This is going to be a great season of television!"

I nodded until Matt leaned forward and disconnected us from the call.

"Well?" he asked, looking at me. "Are you going to say anything?"

"Thank you?"

A cloud crossed Matt's face. "I thought you'd be excited. You love those shows. I thought—" His brow furrowed, and he looked down, away from my face.

Suddenly, the cloud lifted from my brain, and I realized that no matter how uncertain I was about going on TV, Matt had planned this for me. It was a kind and thoughtful gesture. I reached out and grabbed his hand.

"I can't believe you did this for me."

His face lit up with relief. "You had me scared there for a minute, Franny. I thought you were going to tell her no."

Was that an option? It hadn't occurred to me. If it had... well, it was a good thing it hadn't.

"No, of course not. I'm just flattered—and honored. I know I said it already, but I can't believe you did all this."

He took my hand in both of his. "You're an amazing baker, Franny. Every bit as amazing as the ones on TV. I don't care if you think you're just a coffee shop owner. You're amazing. Everything about you is amazing. I don't know what I've done to deserve you."

For the briefest second, I thought I saw tears in his eyes, but then they were gone. Matt wasn't a crier anyway.

He pulled me toward him and kissed me softly then smiled. "I love you, Franny."

"I love you too." We gazed into each other's eyes for a few moments in full romantic-comedy fashion. "So, I guess this is why you've been so secretive lately?"

Matt looked briefly confused and startled before smiling. "You noticed that, huh?"

"How could I not? You were slamming your computer closed every time I walked into the room. If I didn't know you better, I would have been really worried." I paused for a moment then admitted the truth. "Okay, I actually was really worried. I knew you were up to something, but I didn't know what.

And then Gail showed up, and my imagination kind of went crazy. And then Sammy and Rhonda were acting weird, and I just—" I sighed, waving my hands in the air in the best approximation of my crazy brain that I could muster.

"Oh, Franny." He kissed me again. "You have nothing to worry about, I promise. I'm in love with you, and nothing is ever going to change that. Especially not Gail. She's not my type."

I swatted at his chest, and he pulled me close. I snuggled in against him, grateful to feel the strength of his body against me and know that he was mine.

"I don't think I could have pulled off the surprise without Sammy and Rhonda's help, though."

I looked up at him. "Wait, so—"

He grinned. "You'll probably need to make some more videos if you're hoping to post some on social media. The Baking Network requires a video audition, and that was the cover story Sammy and I came up with." He spilled every detail—every phone call with Sammy, every passing conversation with Rhonda, every time he'd asked me a question that the Baking Network had asked him but he didn't know the answer to. "I hated lying to you, but I figured it was for a good cause." He looked at me sheepishly, his warm brown eyes melting any reservations I had about the situation.

I cupped his face in my hands. "It was for a very good cause. I forgive you." I leaned in and kissed him, softly at first and then more intently.

Later that night, I lay in my bed, Matt snoring softly beside me and Latte accompanying him from where he insisted on wedging himself between us. I'd tried but couldn't sleep. The events of the day —heck, the events of the last couple of weeks— kept swirling through my head, slotting themselves into my new reality. That time Matt had asked me about my baking inspiration? For the Baking Network. When Sammy asked about my favorite bakes and ingredients while the camera was on me? Baking Network. When Rhonda sounded almost relieved that the thing I was really worried about was Matt being secretive? She knew about the Baking Network. So many oddities from the last few weeks were easily chalked up to Matt's plan to do something nice for me. Something I never in a million years would have done for myself for a variety of reasons, but something nice. And it was flattering that he and my friends had thought I was good enough. And that the Baking Network thought I was good enough! I'd been worried about my relationship with Matt for nothing.

Sleep finally started to creep in. Everything made sense again. I had nothing to worry about. I closed my eyes and rolled onto my side, thinking through the video call with Gail again. It was a huge opportunity for me and the café. Tourists might come to Cape Bay just for my baked goods. And Matt—he had looked so worried when he thought I wasn't happy. The look in his eyes when I'd asked him if that was why he'd been so sneaky.

The look in his eyes...

He'd looked confused. Startled, even. Why would he look startled? Unless he was hiding something else from me.

My eyes snapped open again, my worries back in full force.

Chapter 9

A PRODUCTION ASSISTANT, complete with headset and clipboard, was waiting for me when Matt and I stepped out of a cab in front of a nondescript warehouse in downtown Boston a short two weeks later.

"Francesca Amaro?" My name in her thick South Boston accent came out as something like "Francescamaro."

I nodded. "Yup. You can call me Fran, though."

She made a checkmark on her clipboard and looked at Matt. "Your name?"

"I'm just here with Franny," he said.

Her eyes flicked back to me.

"He's my boyfriend."

She rolled her eyes dramatically and pushed a

73

button on the small electronic box perched on her hip. "I got Francesca Amaro and her boyfriend." She said *boyfriend* like it was a dirty word.

"He doesn't have to come in with me. He can go to the hotel."

She held one finger up at an arm's length as she listened to something coming through her headset. After a moment, she opened the door behind her. "Go straight down the hall. Fourth door on your left."

"Is it okay if Matt comes?"

"Fourth door on your left," she repeated, more slowly.

I glanced at Matt, who shrugged. "I'll take that as a yes."

He hefted both our bags up onto his shoulder— he'd insisted on carrying all of them—and followed me through the open door into a dark hallway that only got darker when the production assistant let the door slam behind us. It barely even looked like a finished building. The walls on both sides were just metal studs with drywall facing the other way. If the girl at the entrance hadn't said my name, I probably would have turned and run back for the door, convinced I'd wandered into a horror movie.

"Fourth door, she said?" I asked as I started somewhat reluctantly down the hall.

"On your left," Matt said loudly in the same flat tone as the girl's accent. He was grinning when I glanced back at him.

The fourth door was propped open and led into another hallway, this one much brighter. I looked at Matt again for reassurance.

"She said the fouahth," he said, still doing his best to sound like he was a Southie native, not the son of Italian immigrants who was brought up on Cape Cod.

I turned in to the second hallway. There were voices coming from somewhere in the distance, so I headed toward them, still hoping I was on the right path.

Gail popped out of a doorway toward the end of the hall. "Fran! And Matt! Come on back!" She waved us toward her with a huge smile on her face.

We followed her into a large room in which small groups of people were scattered around. "Fran, if you'll come with me. Matt, you can wait over there for one of the PAs to come talk to you and any other partners who come."

Matt hesitated. "Partners?" I could see his mind

whirling at the possibility of having inadvertently signed himself up to help me bake.

Gail laughed loudly and waved her hand in the air. "You know, spouses, boyfriends—it's just easier to call you all 'partners.' Then I don't have to worry about who's what! Now, come on, Fran! Let's meet the other bakers!"

She slipped her arm through mine and dragged me off behind her toward another group of people. Matt slowly and almost dejectedly walked to the empty corner Gail had directed him toward.

"We have another baker," Gail called in a singsong voice as we walked up to a loose group of two women and one man.

The two women stood next to each other while the man stood off to the side, fiddling with his phone. One of the women smiled at me, and the other nodded with a passive expression, but the man barely glanced up from his scrolling and tapping. "Everybody, this is Fran. She's from down in Cape Bay! I'll leave you all to get to know each other."

She dropped my arm and hurried back in the opposite direction. I smiled at my fellow bakers and raised my hand in a half-hearted wave. In true reality TV tradition, I wasn't there to make friends, but I wasn't there to *not* make friends either. I was barely there to win. I just wanted to bake and get it over with.

"I'm Kaitlin." The woman who had smiled at me before was the one who introduced herself now. I said hello, and then there was an uncomfortable silence as neither of the other bakers introduced themselves. Finally, Kaitlin spoke up. "This is Suzette, and that's Winston."

Suzette nodded in my direction. She was gorgeous, with a mass of fiery-red hair so thick and full that it made my hair—the thickness of which I routinely got comments from new hairstylists on—seem lank. Winston, tall and thin with glasses and a checked shirt that looked more at home in an engineering office than a bakeshop, seemed to flick his eyes up from his phone for a fraction of a second, but that was all the acknowledgment I got.

Kaitlin sidled up to me. She was petite, blond, and completely adorable, with big brown eyes ringed by thick lashes. "So, you're from Cape Bay? I love it down there. It's so peaceful."

I agreed, and we chatted for a few minutes. Well, Kaitlin did most of the chatting while I nodded and interjected every so often. She was from a tiny town in the middle of the state between

Worcester and Amherst and worked as a medical transcriptionist by day. By night, she was semifamous online for the elaborate cakes she made and posted pictures of.

"Have we met before?" I asked after a little while. She looked and sounded so familiar, but I knew I didn't follow her online.

Kaitlin blushed and ducked her head. "I was on *Sweet Spring Fling* last year, if you watch that?"

"Oh, that's it!" As soon as she said it, I remembered seeing her on the Baking Network's annual spring show. I also remembered the gorgeous three-tier cake she'd made, completely covered in edible flowers. I still didn't know how she hadn't won with that cake. The flavor of the cake she lost to must have been incredible, because its decoration hadn't held a candle to hers.

"That cake was stunning! You're so talented."

Her blush deepened. "Thanks. I was really proud of it."

"I can't believe you came back for another show with Jeremy Johnson. We're just filming one episode, and I'm dreading it. He's so mean."

She shrugged. "He's not so bad once you get used to him."

I had serious doubts about that, but she was the

one who'd worked with him before, so I'd have to take her word for it. At least until I had the chance to meet the man myself.

I looked around the room. Matt was still standing in the corner alone. Apparently, no other "partners" were coming. Aside from him and the four of us bakers, everyone else standing around looked ready for work—headsets, clipboards, chef's coats. But they all looked vaguely bored, most of them looking around the room like I was. No one seemed to be in charge, and Gail was nowhere to be found. I turned back to Kaitlin. "Do you know what we're waiting for?"

"I'm not sure? More bakers, maybe?"

"How many of us are there going to be?" Some of the Baking Network shows had as many as twelve bakers, but those went on for weeks, and we were only filming one episode. At least, that was what Matt and Gail had led me to believe. I suddenly had visions of being stuck in Boston filming for two months and thought about bolting for the door.

"I'm not sure. Not too many more, probably."

I sighed and rubbed my palms on my jeans nervously as I glanced around some more. "Any tips for a Baking Network rookie?"

Kaitlin grinned. "Oh, lots!"

But before she could share any, Gail came in, trailed by a ridiculously good-looking man with a full head of thick, glossy hair and the kind of face that sold out movie theaters.

"Our final baker is here! Everybody, this is Eduardo. If you give me a couple minutes to get some things organized, we can get this show on the road!" She clapped her hands together and grinned at us then spun on her heel and took off to organize whatever it was she had to organize.

"I am Eduardo," he said in a sultry accent. A smile curved his full lips as he turned to me. "What is your name?"

"Francesca." I didn't know why I said my full name, but it was what came out of my mouth.

"Francesca," he repeated. "A beautiful name for a beautiful woman." He turned to Kaitlin and asked her name.

She smiled at him as if he was water in a desert and told him.

"Kaitlin," he murmured. "So lovely." He turned to Suzette. "And you?"

Suzette did not look remotely charmed by Eduardo's good looks and suave demeanor. She put her hand out to shake. "My name is Suzette."

Her voice had a coldness to it that only momentarily slowed down Eduardo's charm offensive. He smiled after the briefest hesitation. "Suzette. It is a pleasure to meet you." He took her hand in a move that was more a caress than a shake.

She snatched her hand back with a look of disgust. She pointedly turned away from him. Eduardo looked back at me and Kaitlin with a charming smile and a shrug that seemed to acknowledge his failure to win over Suzette.

"I'm Winston."

I was startled to hear Winston's voice. It was deep and resonant and seemed completely out of place coming out of his mouth. Winston had his surprisingly large hand extended in Eduardo's direction. I couldn't help but wonder if there was a reason Winston had more or less ignored me when I arrived but was going out of his way to introduce himself to Eduardo now. I knew some men had strong views about a woman's place—or lack thereof—in the kitchen, but I'd thought that view had mostly gone out of fashion by now. I added Winston to the list of reasons I was unhappy about being here.

Eduardo smiled sheepishly at me and Kaitlin before taking Winston's hand. This time, there was no caressing going on. Winston's eyes bored into Eduardo as he clenched his hand. Eduardo chuckled uncomfortably and moved to pull his hand back, but Winston held on, only letting go after Eduardo seemed to give in. Winston's face noticeably softened as soon as he let go of Eduardo. He looked at me, Kaitlin, and Suzette, giving us a slight nod, then went back to his phone. Maybe it wasn't women he had a problem with—maybe it was men. Or maybe just Eduardo. I'd only known him about two minutes, but I could see how his mannerisms could easily cross the line from charming to sleazy.

Kaitlin and I exchanged a surprised look. I was glad to see that she had noticed the odd interaction as well.

Out of the corner of my eye, I saw one of the people in headsets approach Matt. She gestured a bunch, and then he gestured in my direction, then she did, then they started walking over.

He put his arm around my waist and pulled me slightly away from the group with a pointed look at Eduardo. So he'd noticed Eduardo's smooth moves as well.

"She's going to take me over to the hotel to check in. I guess you guys have some stuff to do, so I'll catch up to you later, okay?"

I nodded my agreement, and he pulled me in for a kiss—a much longer and slower kiss than we would normally exchange in public. He gave Eduardo another look before walking away.

I was blushing as I stepped back to the group of bakers.

"He is a very passionate man, your husband," Eduardo said with a twinkle in his eye.

"Boyfriend," I muttered.

"Not for long, I think."

I gave him a look. What did he mean, "not for long"? Did he think Matt kissing me in public was him covering up for something? I shook the thought from my head. I had literally just met Eduardo. For all I knew, he was a total sleazeball who enjoyed making women feel insecure about their partners and then moving in for the metaphorical kill.

Fortunately, Gail showed back up before I could stew about it any longer. "All right!" She clapped her hands together a couple of times in a combination of a ready-to-go gesture and an attempt to get our attention. The room, never that loud to begin with, quieted down, and everybody turned to face Gail. "Are we ready to get this show on the road?" There was some half-hearted cheering from the production people and Kaitlin. Gail turned and said something to the man with a clipboard beside her. She spoke quietly, but I just barely caught the words "energy up."

She turned back to us with a big smile. "For any of you who don't know, I'm Gail Malinsky, and I'm the executive producer on the Baking Network's newest series, *Hometown Showdown!*" There was another smattering of cheers, and Gail looked again at the man next to her, who nodded before she could even say anything. "We're going to have a super-exciting couple of days working together! Our judges won't be joining us until we start filming tomorrow, but I'm thrilled to let you know that we have the honor to be joined by Jeremy Johnson and Veronica Browning."

It was the first I'd heard that Veronica Browning would also be a judge on the show, and I'd have been lying if I said I wasn't a little excited. She'd been a child actress before becoming a rock star's wife and then getting her own show on the Baking Network a few years earlier. When I was a kid, her show had been my absolute favorite. She was only about five years older than me, and I loved watching the antics of her sassy character and the myriad ways she tried to get out of trouble. Somehow, when I tried those same tricks in real life, they never seemed to work out as well for me as they did for her. Still, I had lived for the new episodes of her show each Friday night. I couldn't believe that after all these years, I was finally going to get to meet her in person.

"Before we get started, I want to remind you all that we are going to be *on TV*, which is really exciting!" She paused and looked at all of us with wide eyes. Kaitlin started to clap but then glanced around at the rest of us and slowly dropped her hands. Gail looked perturbed. "Millions of people at home would kill to be in your shoes, so let's make sure we keep our energy up to show everyone how happy we are to be here, okay?"

This time, Kaitlin glanced around at all of us before clapping or cheering. We weren't, so she didn't. Gail was starting to look twitchy. "Okay. We'll work on our energy more later." She glanced again at the man beside her. He nodded and scribbled on his clipboard. She clapped her hands again, this time giving the sense that she was trying to psych herself up to deal with our stubborn reticence. "So, we have a busy couple days! The episode that airs may only be one hour, but it takes a lot longer than that to film, doesn't it, Neil?"

"It sure does, Gail!" The man beside her spoke

up for the first time, as if on cue. "I have call sheets here for each of you, listing what times you'll need to be here for filming. It may seem like a lot, but don't worry. It's only three days!" He chuckled, if you could call it that. It was a forced sound that seemed like it was as much a part of the script as everything else he'd said.

He walked over to us and handed each of us a sheet of paper. I scanned down it to see a detailed list of times over the next three days that I would be filming or available for filming. I was more or less booked for sixteen hours a day. And here I had thought participating in the show would be a little bit of a vacation. Matt had clearly thought so, too, based on the puppy-dog eyes he'd given me when he'd asked if it was all right if he came with me so we could have a romantic getaway. So much for that.

Neil had finished handing out the papers and gone back to stand beside Gail, who had resumed talking, giving some more details about what the production staff had in store for us. It sounded exhausting, and yet again, I considered just walking out but knew it would hurt Matt's feelings and probably send Gail into a tizzy. I'd only just met them, but I felt bad about inflicting that on my fellow bakers. And who knew who she'd draft in my place? Did she have a replacement waiting in the wings, or would she draft some poor production assistant to fill in? Or was everyone so eager to be on TV that they'd never had to consider the possibility of a last-minute replacement before? I would stay. I was stuck.

"So, let's go take a look at the space that will be your kitchen, and then you'll each meet with hair and makeup before we wrap for the day!"

Gail led our group into an adjoining room that was swarming with people working on—well, it seemed like everything. "This, bakers, is your kitchen! Or it will be soon, anyway!" She forced a chuckle that sounded as scripted as Neil's had. I wondered how many times they'd done this routine. "Because *Hometown Showdown* films on location in each city we're featuring, we have to set up and break down the entire kitchen every. Single. Time. But don't worry, bakers. Everything will be running smoothly and in working order by the time you walk in tomorrow!"

She gave us a brief tour of the space that she claimed would be a kitchen in the morning, even though I couldn't fathom how that was possible. The space was a disaster area. There were small sections covered in faux-woodgrain vinyl planks and large areas that were still bare concrete floor. A cluster of what looked like small kitchen islands was off to the side, and the room rang with the sound of power tools and cords slapping the bare floor as workers yanked and hauled them in different directions. Calling it chaos was generous.

The PA who'd greeted Matt and me at the door hurried up to Gail and whispered something in her ear. Gail looked annoyed but plastered another smile on her face and clapped her hands again. "Well, bakers, we have a little change of plan. Hair and makeup aren't quite ready for you yet, so we're going to give you a little break and bus you back to the hotel. A PA will come by each of your rooms when we're ready for you."

We followed Neil through a maze of corridors and out a door, where a minivan waited for us. He herded us all in, gave some directions to the driver, and waved goodbye as we headed off to the hotel.

Chapter 10

IN THE HOTEL ROOM, I filled Matt in on everything that had happened at the warehouse-cum-studio and warned him about my lengthy filming schedule. We had just started getting cozy when a PA knocked on the door and requested my presence back on set.

With a sigh from me and puppy-dog eyes from Matt, I smoothed my clothes and hair, put my shoes back on, and headed down to the lobby. Eduardo, Winston, and Suzette were already there, standing in an awkward group. Despite her not being the friendliest person I'd ever met, I was glad Suzette was there. The idea of having to make small talk with Eduardo and Winston wasn't exactly appealing. I went and stood next to her. "Not much of a break, huh?"

She shrugged vaguely. "I'm used to being busy in the kitchen all day. I rarely have any time to rest."

"Oh, same. My café is always crazy, especially this time of year." I didn't know why I felt compelled to impress her or at least convince her we were equally busy and important, but I did.

It didn't seem to be working.

She sniffed dismissively but didn't turn away, so at least there was that.

The elevator nearby dinged, and the door opened. The PA and Kaitlin stepped out, the PA looking like she was not enjoying her job or life very much at the moment and Kaitlin looking like she'd just woken up from a nap.

"Let's go, folks." The PA didn't even stop, just motioned at us and walked toward the door. We followed behind her like good little ducks.

We piled back into the same minivan with the PA in the driver's seat, Eduardo beside her, and Winston and Suzette in the middle captain's chairs, and somehow, Kaitlin and I ended up climbing in the back.

"You okay?" I asked, leaning over to her as we pulled out of the hotel driveway.

"Just sleepy." She yawned.

"Hopefully, this won't take too long." I tried to sound encouraging, but I wasn't sure it worked.

"Did you see that schedule? It looks exhausting! I don't know how I'm going to make it."

I nodded. "It's brutal."

We fell into friendly silence for the rest of the short ride to the set, or at least, I thought we did until everyone else had gotten out of the van and Kaitlin didn't move to follow. I turned back. "Kaitlin?"

She shook her head and looked up, looking startled and sleepy.

"We're here."

She looked confused.

"At the set. For hair and makeup."

I could see the mental gears click into place.

"Oh!" She scrambled out of the back seat, rubbing her eyes. She fell in next to me as we followed the PA into the building. "Thanks. It feels like I've been falling asleep every time I sit down lately."

I nodded sympathetically. If she was being serious, she probably needed to see a doctor, but I wasn't going to say that to someone who was basically a stranger.

The PA walked us through the hallways until we popped out into a room that, based on the construction noises coming through the wall beside us, seemed to be right on the other side of the kitchen they were building for us. Two women were in the room, both dressed in black and wearing apron-like tool belts and big, bright smiles.

"Hey, y'all, I'm Jaleesa." Jaleesa wore bright-pink lipstick, coppery eyeshadow, and the tight coils of her hair pulled back in a ponytail. "I'm gonna help y'all with your makeup."

"And I'm Marissa. I'm here for hair." Marissa, too, wore her hair in a ponytail, but hers was long and sleek. "Jaleesa and I will meet with each of you to get to know you a little bit and figure out how we're going to style you for filming." She turned to Jaleesa. "Who do you want to start with?"

"Let's get the guys done, and then we can focus on you beautiful ladies." She winked at us, and then the PA whisked us away to the green room, where we'd apparently be spending our downtime.

It wasn't long before I got called back down to the hair-and-makeup room. Marissa greeted me with a smile as I settled into her chair.

She pulled my hair back behind my shoulders.

"So, how do you like to wear your hair while you bake?"

I demonstrated the simple chignon I usually twisted my hair into for work, then she combed it out with her fingers and started recreating the hairstyle herself.

"I didn't realize we'd have hair and makeup."

Marissa smiled at me in the mirror. "It's just a little bit. We want you guys to look like yourselves, but between the TV lights and needing you guys to look the same both days—and all day—they like to give you a little professional help." She twisted a thick lock of my hair around her finger and held it against my head. "At least this time, casting solved my biggest problem for me!"

I tried to imagine how casting could solve a hair-and-makeup problem but couldn't. "What's your biggest problem?"

She met my eyes in the mirror again. "Do you know how much three brunette white girls can look alike when they all have their hair done the same? Girl. We need to make sure viewers can glance at the screen and know exactly who's who. I was thrilled when I saw that I had a blonde, a brunette, a redhead, a tall black guy, and a short Latin guy. No one's mixing you all up."

It was a point I hadn't really thought of before, but it made sense. Matt was constantly mixing up the two male leads on my favorite TV drama. He swore they looked exactly alike, but their only similarity was that they both had short brown hair.

Marissa finished styling my hair, shoved about forty bobby pins into it, and secured it all with what seemed like half a can of hair spray. "Shake your head," she instructed.

I shook it. Not a single hair moved. She declared it perfect and sent me over to Jaleesa, who coated my face in water- and sweat-resistant products that she assured me would stay in place through a whole day of baking.

Eduardo held a finger to his lips as I walked back into the green room. He pointed over at the couch on the other side of the room, where Kaitlin was curled up in a little ball, sound asleep. She really did seem to fall asleep every time she sat down.

I took another chair and pulled out my phone to send a few texts to Matt and Sammy to update them on what had been going on and, in Sammy's case, see how things were going at the café. Despite the fact that I knew Sammy was more than capable of running things on her own, I was still worried about all the little day-to-day things I usually took care of, like ordering napkins. Did we have enough napkins? We always seemed to need more napkins. Sammy ended up sending me a picture of her serious expression with Rhonda photobombing her in the background making a silly face. Apparently, they did not appreciate my questions.

I forced myself to put my phone down and just sit quietly. Who knew how much quiet time I'd have over the next few days? I should appreciate it now while I had it.

Suzette came back into the room after about ten minutes. Her red curls were now held back off her face with a thick headband, but otherwise, she looked the same after her visit to hair and makeup.

Eduardo signaled to her to be quiet as he'd done with me. She barely acknowledged him as she took a seat on the opposite side of the room. I wondered how long we were going to let Kaitlin sleep and if there was something else we were supposed to be doing. What if production had given Kaitlin instructions before she'd fallen asleep and now none of us knew that we were supposed to be doing something important because we didn't want to disturb her rest?

I took a deep breath. "Relax, Fran," I whispered. It wasn't something I was good at, but I was going to have to chill out and not try to control the situation. I wasn't in charge. It wasn't my job. I took another deep, slow breath like I was in yoga class and focused on my breathing. Or tried to, anyway. I still hadn't managed to fully relax when the same production assistant who had fetched us from our hotel rooms appeared in the doorway.

"Let's load up in the van for dinner." She waved her hand toward the door.

I was surprised when Suzette gently woke Kaitlin. She'd seem so standoffish so far that I hadn't expected that kind of tenderness from her.

I lingered toward the back of the group as we filed out of the room so I could talk to the PA without holding everyone up.

"Excuse me," I started, sidling up to her. "My boyfriend's here, too, and——"

"This dinner is for bakers only and is mandatory. There will be other opportunities later for bakers to socialize with other people outside of the group." She sounded as if she was reciting from a script, and I wondered again how many times they'd all done this specific routine, just in a different city with a different group of bakers. I supposed that it was like my own daily routine in some ways. I just hoped I didn't seem as bored with mine when talking to other people.

I texted Matt from the van to go ahead and eat without me. He was disappointingly okay with it because he'd just figured out that one of his buddies from college lived in the neighborhood. Matt would just grab dinner with him. I didn't need to hurry back or anything. He and his buddy would be fine. I put my phone back in my pocket and stared glumly out the window. Matt had come on this trip so we could spend time together, and he didn't even seem the slightest bit disappointed that our romantic weekend was going up in smoke.

To my surprise, the van pulled up in front of the hotel again. I wondered if I'd misunderstood the timeline or if we were supposed to get changed for dinner, but no one else asked, so neither did I.

The PA hopped out of the driver's seat, handed the keys to the valet, and walked around to open the van door for us. "Go straight inside and hang a left," she said as we climbed out.

I realized then that we were eating in the hotel restaurant. "Are you sure my boyfriend can't—"

"Bakers only." She pushed the button to close the minivan door and walked past me into the hotel.

I told myself it was fine since Matt already had other plans, but I was still a little annoyed at the way she'd cut me off.

Inside the restaurant, we were shown to a table already set for five. The PA spoke briefly to the restaurant manager then came over to the table. "Dinner is paid for by production. No more than twenty dollars per person. When you're done, you can go up to your rooms. Call time is at six, so the van will be here for you at five forty-five. We're on a strict schedule, so try not to be late." The last part of her instruction sounded distinctly like she was already annoyed with us and fully expected to wake up at least one of us, probably more. It wasn't the most personable send-off, but I was quickly learning that television wasn't the friendliest business.

The dinner ended up being quite pleasant, although the prices at the restaurant combined with the twenty-dollar limit meant the only thing any of us could get was a burger. It was a decent burger but not as good as the ones Matt and I got from our burger joint in Cape Bay.

Eduardo turned out to be funny in addition to charming. Suzette and Winston actually talked, which was a surprise based on how quiet they'd been so far. They seemed to know each other too.

Kaitlin was sweet and pleasant and somehow managed to stay awake the whole time.

We were having such a good time that it was eleven o'clock before we realized that the restaurant was shutting down around us. That six a.m. call time was going to be painful.

I headed up to the room, hoping to get a few minutes to talk to Matt before I had to go to bed if I was going to be at all functional in the morning. But when I opened the door, Matt was already sprawled out on the bed, sound asleep.

Chapter 11

THE NEXT DAY was a frantic dash of hurry up and wait.

We all actually managed to make it to the van on time without anyone having to come look for any of us. They ferried us to the set, where we sat for almost an hour before anyone came to tell us there was breakfast waiting for us in an adjoining room. An hour after *that*, Jaleesa and Marissa came to get us. Their hands practically flew around our heads as they got us each ready for our first on-camera work. Of course, once they got us ready, we spent another hour sitting in the green room, waiting for someone to come get us.

I was the first one called back. I was shown a rack of brightly colored aprons that I recognized from other Baking Network shows and told to pick one. I chose one in a pretty blue that I thought would bring out my eyes. Once I had it on, one of the production assistants led me down a hall and around a corner into the kitchen. To my surprise, it actually looked like a kitchen. The workers were gone, and everything looked like it did on TV— except it was missing one whole wall. I'd never noticed it before, but it made sense that they needed the space for the camera.

Gail and Neil, along with a woman at the camera and a sound guy holding a big fur-covered microphone, were waiting for me. Gail smiled. "Hi, Fran! We're going to start by filming introductions. If you can just go stand on that taped X in the middle of the floor."

I went and stood on the spot she'd indicated.

"Now smile, and say your name and where you're from. Big energy, Fran! Action!"

I pasted on a smile. "Hi! I'm Francesca Amaro, and I'm from Cape Bay, Massachusetts."

There was a long pause while I waited for someone to say "cut" or anything at all.

Finally, Gail sighed. "Let's try it again. High energy, please, Fran. Whenever you're ready. We're still rolling."

I did it again, this time trying to sound more cheerful and energetic. Apparently, I did not succeed.

Gail looked at Neil. He walked over to me and leaned in conspiratorially. "We're looking for really high energy here, Fran. Anything less doesn't translate on TV. Remember, you're thrilled to be on the Baking Network. Now watch." He turned to face the camera and stepped forward with ballerina posture and a smile so wide it looked painful. "I'm Neil Waterman, and I'm from Los Angeles, California!"

I sighed. I didn't know if I had that much enthusiasm in me. He sounded like a cheerleader or a beauty pageant contestant.

"Can we try it like that?" he asked, reverting to his normal, sedate self.

It was then that I realized it was just an act. It was reality TV, but it was still acting.

I nodded. "I'll try."

He put his hand on my shoulder. "Don't try. Just do it."

I nodded again. If I ever wanted to get finished, I was going to have to.

I waited for him to take his place back behind Gail and then for her to nod and point at me.

I threw my head and shoulders back and smiled as widely as I could. "I'm Francesca Amaro! And I'm from Cape Bay, Massachusetts!"

"That's perfect!" Gail beamed at me. "Now one more time, just to make sure we have the shot."

I repeated my introduction with even more enthusiasm, and Gail sent me back to the green room, where I waited for a couple of hours while the other bakers cycled in and out, filming their own introductions. Then the cycle started over with each of us being called into another room to film our first "confessionals," which involved us sitting with a producer and a camera and answering questions. It felt a little bit like being in elementary school again, having to answer questions in complete sentences and restating the questions. When the producer asked my favorite things to bake, I couldn't just answer with "cakes and pies." I had to say, "My favorite things to bake are cakes and pies." And say it with cheerleader-level enthusiasm, but not too much, because with the camera so close, too much enthusiasm could come off as fake.

After we spent a few more hours waiting in the green room and made a few trips to craft services to get snacks, Gail and Neil finally came to gather us all for a tour of the kitchen we'd be working in. We made our way around the large room, having each convection oven, deep fryer, ice cream maker, blast freezer, ingredient rack, and other piece of equipment explained to us. It seemed like a lot of information and instruction for a competition to see who could make the best Boston cream pie. But at this point, I had resigned myself to being along for the ride.

Our tour concluded at one of the baker's stations. There, we each had our own traditional oven, a stovetop, and a stand mixer.

"Now, bakers, I want you to take special note of the pots, pans, and utensils you each have at your stations." Gail held up a mixing spoon with a blue silicone handle. "These are from our new Baking Network Home line—professional-quality tools for the home baker. We want you all to really show how much you enjoy using them and how high quality they are. Kaitlin, it would be especially good if you could focus on that since you're a home baker."

"I use professional tools at home." Kaitlin looked slightly offended. I couldn't blame her. She might not have had a day job, but she was hugely popular online and had already been successful on another Baking Network show.

Gail smiled at her. "I know that, of course. But the viewers at home don't. And they love to root for the underdog"—at this, Kaitlin looked even more offended—"so you being a home baker really gets them on your side." If Gail noticed Kaitlin's scowl, she didn't give any indication. She just plowed ahead in her speech. "You each have a knife block full of Baking Network Home knives with our signature blue handle. These knife blocks come with every kind of knife a baker could need at home, including"—she pulled one of the knives from the block with a flourish as we all stepped back—"a palette knife for icing your cakes!"

I had never heard of a palette knife being included in a knife block, but I could see how it could be a nice inclusion for a home baker stocking their kitchen for the first time.

"So, do any of you have any questions?" Gail looked expectantly at the group of us.

"We can't use our own tools?" Suzette asked.

Gail frowned. "No, I'm sorry. It's very important that you use the tools provided, both so that everyone is on an equal playing field and so that we can show everyone how good the new Baking Network Home tools are."

Suzette heaved an annoyed sigh. I thought I saw

her exchange a look with Winston, too, but I wasn't sure.

"Does anyone have any other questions?" Gail scanned our faces. "No? Okay, then, I'll let you all get some food and some rest! It's been a long day, and we start bright and early tomorrow morning! Remember, you are welcome to bring a notebook with your recipes in it, but no cell phones or other electronic devices! We can't have any extra noise during filming, and besides, it's the only way to keep it fair. It's absolutely fine to do research before the competition begins, but that research needs to be done before the cameras start rolling. Okay? Okay! Now, you all have a great night, and I'll see you in the morning!"

Gail left us with Neil, who escorted us to the door. We waited for several minutes before the minivan finally pulled up with a new driver.

"Is dinner tonight in the same restaurant?" Eduardo asked the driver when we were almost at the hotel.

"You're on your own for dinner tonight. You can go out or get room service."

Eduardo swiveled in the front seat to look at the rest of us. "We should go out, yes? Experience some of the food this fine city has to offer? Better than room service."

"I'm down for that," Winston said.

Suzette nodded beside him.

I glanced at Kaitlin, who was dozing beside me, and nudged her. "Do you want to go out for dinner or get room service?" I fully expected her to say she wanted to get room service, but she said she wanted to go out. If she had declined to go out, I would have, too, in hopes that Matt and I could go out. "Kaitlin and I will go too," I announced to the van. I waited a beat and then asked, "Does anyone mind if my boyfriend comes along?"

"No, not at all!" Eduardo answered for everyone. "It will be good to see him again."

My cheeks felt warm as I remembered how Matt had made a point the day before to kiss me in front of Eduardo and the other bakers. I tried to ignore it and pulled my phone out of my pocket to text Matt. We'd messaged back and forth a few times during the day. To my dismay, he didn't seem to be missing me too much. He'd spent the day with his friend from college again, and they were already planning to go see a Red Sox game while I was filming tomorrow. I didn't blame him for going to a baseball game, but I couldn't deny that our trip wasn't really working out the way I'd envisioned.

Going out to dinner with the other bakers. Want to join us?

I watched the screen, hoping he'd text back quickly. Sure enough, he did.

Already out at dinner with Chris and some of his friends. Sorry babe.

I tried to stuff down my disappointment, blinking back the tears that had instantly filled my eyes.

Kaitlin's hand patted mine, and I looked over to see her regarding me sympathetically.

Chapter 12

"ALL RIGHT, is everyone on their marks?"

The five of us bakers looked down at our feet to make sure we were all standing on the tape marks assigned to us. It was midmorning the next day, and we'd all been through wardrobe, hair, and makeup to make sure we looked exactly the same as we had when we'd filmed our introductions the day before. Now we were in a carefully arranged huddle, with Kaitlin and Eduardo standing a few feet apart and Winston, me, and Suzette staggered behind them so the camera could get us all in one shot. After two days on set, we were finally getting ready to actually bake.

Neil continued, "We're going to bring in the judges in just a minute. We want you all to show us how excited you are to meet them and to be here on Baking Network. How about you show us that now?"

I did my best to look happy and excited, having already learned that we would have to try again until we made it up to Neil and Gail's standards. From the looks on their faces, we were not achieving it.

Neil looked over at Gail, who was seated beside one of the three cameras currently trained on us. She made a small upward gesture with her hand.

"Let's try that again!" Neil said, the smile on his face clearly not what he was feeling inside. "Can we get a cheer? Some clapping? Remember, we're happy to be here and excited to meet Veronica Browning and the one and only Jeremy Johnson!"

I smiled bigger and clapped a little. Mentioning Veronica Browning actually had something of the effect Neil was looking for, at least with me. I generally subscribed to the theory that you should never meet your heroes, but I didn't have a choice at this point, so I just leaned into my nervous excitement.

Neil seemed happy with our enthusiasm this time around. "Once more for the cameras!"

We clapped again. Kaitlin cheered gamely.

"Without looking at the cameras, Eduardo.

Look straight forward toward me. Remember, never look at the cameras except in confessionals or when you're asked to." Neil paused to let us cheer yet again. "Good, good! Now let's take five to reset the cameras. Bakers, you can go to the green room or craft services, but don't wander far—this is just a short break!" He clapped his hands, and there was a flurry of activity as production assistants and camera people swarmed the set to make adjustments.

We bakers headed backstage. While the rest of our group headed for the couches in the green room, Kaitlin and I peeled off to head toward the snack table. "You okay?" I asked, noticing Kaitlin looked a little green around the gills.

"Hmm? Yeah. Just a little nervous, I guess." She grabbed a few apple slices and some crackers from the table. Definitely a nervous stomach.

I added some grapes and apples to my plate, wanting to keep things light since I'd be on my feet all day. We found some chairs nearby and sat to eat.

"Any last-minute tips?" I asked, trying to make conversation and maybe take her mind off her nerves.

She smiled gratefully. "Try to forget the cameras are there. Not just so you don't look at them but because it's a lot of pressure if you start thinking about all the people watching at home. It's easier just to pretend you're cooking in your own kitchen."

"Don't you bake on camera a lot?"

Kaitlin nodded. "Yeah, but it's different when it's just you and your phone. Even when you're going live, so there are actually people watching what you're doing, it's easy to forget when it's just you in your kitchen doing what you love. When there's an actual huge camera hovering over you and producers wandering around, it's a lot harder to get into the zone and focus on your baking."

"Bakers to the set, please! Bakers to the set!" Neil's voice seemed to come out of nowhere.

I tossed my last couple grapes into my mouth and stood up. Kaitlin looked at her plate for a second then put the crackers in her apron pocket. I admired her commitment to her snacks. We tossed our plates into the trash and headed back to set.

"By the way——" Kaitlin leaned in toward me just before we stepped on the set. "Don't be afraid of Jeremy. He's a really good man once you get to know him."

I nodded, slightly puzzled by her choice of words, but chalked it up to her nerves.

We took our places back on our pieces of tape.

Gail called action. And finally, they walked out, Jeremy Johnson and Veronica Browning.

The first thing I noticed was how handsome Jeremy Johnson was in person. Far, far more handsome than showed on TV. His eyes scanned our group, and my heart skipped a little when they landed on mine.

The next thing I noticed was that the camera did not undersell Veronica in the same way. Time had not been her friend. And neither, frankly, had the plastic surgeon's knife. For the most part, it was subtle, and I couldn't quite explain it. Her skin was pulled taut, a little too smooth, a little too shiny, but you could still see the age. Her lips and cheeks were just a little too puffy. Her hair even looked a little too crispy, and while it had a shine under the lights, I had the feeling that it was more due to some high-end product Marissa had added to it than to natural good health. I should have stuck with not meeting my heroes.

"Bakers, look excited! You're thrilled to meet our judges!"

For once, I didn't mind being told how to feel. I was grateful to have something to focus on other than the judges' looks. I smiled, clasped my hands in front of my chest, and tried not to meet Jeremy Johnson's beautiful eyes again.

"Veronica, when you're ready." Neil stood off to the side, next to Gail. While she was clearly still in charge, Neil's job seemed to be to keep things rolling.

On cue, Veronica's mouth broke into a smile. Her forehead still didn't move, and her eyes didn't change, but her mouth was definitely in a smile shape. "Bakers, welcome to *Hometown Showdown*, Boston Edition!"

"Perfect, Veronica! Next line when you're ready!"

"I'm Veronica Browning! And beside me, as I'm sure you all know, is the esteemed Jere—" Her voice broke off. "Really, Gail? Not only do I have to introduce him, but I have to fawn over him too?"

"Sorry, Veronica. It's in his contract." Gail sounded tired, as if she'd already had this conversation.

"Why isn't it in *my* contract?"

"Because your agent didn't negotiate for it. Now, let's take it from the introductions." She didn't count or say action again, just waved her finger in the air. Everyone seemed to know what that meant.

Veronica huffed, threw her hair back, and took a step away from Jeremy.

"Back on your mark, please, Veronica."

Reluctantly, Veronica stepped back to where she'd been. She closed her eyes, took a breath, and started again. "I'm Veronica Browning! And beside me, as I'm sure you all know is the *esteemed* Jeremy Johnson." She put a lot of emphasis on the word "esteemed," and I wondered if her disdain would show on TV.

If Jeremy noticed it, he gave no indication. He just stood there with his hands in his pockets and a slight smile on his lips. "Welcome, bakers. We're looking forward to tasting your bakes." Jeremy's voice also sounded much better in person than it did on TV. It was low and warm, and I could already see why Kaitlin had made it a point to talk him up.

It was Veronica's turn again. "Your first challenge is simple. Just make us the best Boston cream pie you can. That's not so hard, is it?"

"Just remember, bakers, with a cake as simple as this one, there's nowhere to hide any mistakes. We don't expect much, just perfection."

"And, no pressure, but remember that you're competing for *ten thousand dollars* and the chance to have your recipe printed on Baking Network's website."

I didn't know if that was the first time I'd heard what the prize was or if it was just the first time I really processed it, but I was momentarily stunned by the thought of all that money. It would be huge for me. I could think of all kinds of improvements that I could make to the café with that money. Or my house! I loved my house, but it could stand to be modernized a little. Nothing major, just some things like paint, new carpets, a couple new appliances, maybe a redone bathroom. Suddenly, my competitive juices were flowing, and I wanted to not just get through the competition but win it. I was going to make the best Boston cream pie of my life.

Veronica smiled at us again, or at least did her best to make that shape with her mouth. "So head to your stations and get baking!"

Chapter 13

TWO HOURS OF BAKING LATER—A ridiculously short amount of time to mix, bake, cool, and prepare a cake—we were waiting in the green room for the production assistants to clean up the kitchen before our judging. It felt awkward to have someone else clean up after me, but I reminded myself that I always cleaned up as I went, so my station at least wasn't a disaster. And the PAs were getting paid well to clean up after us. Or at least, I hoped they were.

Being finished with her bake didn't seem to be doing Kaitlin's nerves any favors. She still looked almost green.

"Can I get you a snack or anything, Kaitlin? Some apples or something?" I asked.

She shook her head then froze and clapped her

hand over her mouth. Her eyes looked panicked. I reached for the trash can in the corner beside me, but before I could grab it, Kaitlin lunged forward and vomited into it.

I heard a sharp exhale from the other side of the room and turned to see Suzette looking... distressed, for lack of a better word. Of course, someone throwing up a few feet away from you could do that.

Kaitlin rocked back on her heels, tears in her eyes. "I'm sorry. I'm sorry," she said over and over.

"It's okay. It happens." I grabbed a tissue from the nearby end table and handed it to her then grabbed a handful more, picked up the trash can, and carried it into the hall, where I handed it to a passing PA with an apology. I felt bad leaving him to deal with it, but I wanted to get back to Kaitlin.

Thankfully, Suzette had stepped in to help. The two of them were sitting on the couch. Kaitlin was hunched over, and Suzette was holding a bottle of water, encouraging Kaitlin to take small sips and rinse her mouth out.

I knelt on Kaitlin's other side. "Are you okay?"

She nodded. "I think it's something I ate. Maybe something last night. My fish tasted kind of weird, but I thought it was a seasoning they used."

Suzette raised her eyes and caught mine.

"Do you need to go back to the hotel?" I asked.

Kaitlin shook her head. "No. No, I'm feeling better now. I'll be okay." She leaned back on the sofa and took a deep breath. "I'm okay. I'm okay." She put her head back and closed her eyes.

Suzette and I exchanged another look. I wasn't sure nerves or bad fish were the cause of Kaitlin's nausea, and I was pretty sure Suzette wasn't either. Still, arguing that with Kaitlin wasn't going to make any difference in the situation now.

Suzette sat back next to Kaitlin, and I took a chair nearby. Winston and Eduardo were both on their phones, trying to spare Kaitlin's feelings by looking as if they weren't paying attention, but based on their furtive glances our way, I knew they were.

It wasn't long after that we were called back to the kitchen for judging. Suzette and I walked carefully on either side of Kaitlin. She seemed to be doing better, whether because throwing up had actually cleared her stomach of what was bothering it or through sheer determination.

We took our places on our tape marks. They'd rearranged us for this shot, with me in the front next to Kaitlin, Suzette in between us, and behind, and Winston and Eduardo flanking her. I was glad that Suzette and I were closest to Kaitlin in case we needed to catch her.

Winston was called up to present his cake first. He briefly introduced it, explaining the type of cake he'd used, the particular cream, and the way he'd made his ganache. It was a very traditional Boston cream, and the judges seemed happy with it, although not particularly blown away.

Suzette was next. Her version had an extra-light genoise sponge, a fluffy vanilla mousse, and a chocolate Swiss buttercream icing on top. The judges were complimentary, and Veronica mentioned several times how light and refreshing it was. I expected Suzette to look happy when she turned around, but her eyes were narrowed and her jaw clenched. As soon as she saw me looking, though, the expression faded and returned to a calm, neutral look. Maybe she had been hoping for more praise than she got, but they'd seemed happy enough. Certainly, they seemed to appreciate her less traditional take on it.

I didn't have too much time to think about it as Eduardo was called up next. I was getting more and more nervous the longer I waited, but I took a deep breath and tried to keep calm.

Eduardo had made a Latin-inspired Boston cream. Jeremy and Veronica instantly looked skeptical.

"You know we wanted a classic Boston cream pie, don't you?" Jeremy asked.

"I do, but I think you'll really like this." I couldn't see Eduardo's face from where I stood, but he sounded confident.

Jeremy, on the other hand, looked unsure. Veronica looked pretty much the same as always since her eyebrows didn't really move.

"My Latin-inspired Boston cream is made with a white cake, a dulce de leche custard, and a Mexican chocolate ganache."

Jeremy and Veronica took tentative bites then looked at each other.

"I'm impressed, Eduardo," Veronica said. "It's definitely a Boston cream pie but just a little more decadent and indulgent. Very nice."

Jeremy shared his similarly positive comments, then Eduardo stepped back, and they called Kaitlin up. I swallowed hard, realizing I was going to be last. For better or for worse, my cake was going to be the last one they tasted.

Kaitlin stepped forward and haltingly introduced her cake. I was afraid she still wasn't feeling well. "Um, I made a Boston cream pie." She chuckled quietly. "With a pound cake for the sponge, a, um, pastry cream as the filling, and a chocolate mirror glaze."

We watched as the judges tasted her cake. Jeremy didn't even wait for Veronica to put her fork down before he started in on Kaitlin. "Kaitlin, this is not good."

I heard a sharp intake of air behind me as Suzette gasped.

"First off, your pastry cream is curdled. I can't eat it. I won't eat it. Second, your sponge is dry. It might have been saved by the pastry cream, but, like I said, that's inedible. And then to literally top it off, your mirror glaze—aside from not being well mirrored and quite lumpy down the sides—is like rubber. I feel like I'm chewing on a burnt tire. But somehow, it's also all unbearably sweet. If this is how you bake, I don't know how you got here." He leaned back in his chair and stared at her with an air of defiance.

"Unfortunately, I agree with Jeremy. It's just not good, Kaitlin. I'm sorry." Veronica at least had the decency to try to arrange her surgically fixed features into the shape of regret.

I heard a strangled sob as Kaitlin returned to

stand next to me without waiting to be dismissed. I took her hand and squeezed it then rushed forward before they even called me. I knew the cameras would be on Kaitlin's face, and I wanted to give them something else to film. I couldn't believe the producers let me get away with it.

"Today, I have for you a pretty traditional Boston cream pie. It's a yellow cake brushed with a bourbon syrup. The custard filling also has just a touch of bourbon in it, as does the chocolate ganache on top. Enjoy."

I could hear Kaitlin sniffling behind me. I wanted to go give her a hug, but I kept my back straight and my gaze fixed on the judges. I wasn't going to give Jeremy the satisfaction of showing that he'd rattled me by tearing into Kaitlin.

I couldn't read the judges' faces as they tasted my cake. It would have been nerve-wracking if I hadn't been so upset by what they'd done to Kaitlin. Still, it seemed like an eternity before they rendered their verdict.

"What made you use bourbon, Fran? It's not really a Bostonian ingredient." Jeremy looked at me inscrutably.

"I thought the vanilla notes in this particular bourbon went well with the base flavors of the cake, and the oaky and smoke flavors helped to offset some of the sweetness." I paused for a moment and then shared the real reason. "Plus, my boyfriend is a real bourbon lover, so I thought it would be a nice tribute to him."

Jeremy nodded. "Well, you're lucky that it works as well as it does. It's a really delicious cake."

I couldn't help but smile and was instantly annoyed with myself for it. He'd been so mean to Kaitlin. It felt disloyal to her for me to revel in Jeremy's praise.

He and Veronica complimented my cake some more, almost seeming to be trying to outdo each other with their praise. It only made an uncomfortable situation worse.

When they finally let me rejoin the group of bakers, I took Kaitlin's hand again. She let me but didn't look up.

Gail called "cut," and Neil quickly escorted us from the kitchen. I had a feeling the speed at which it had all happened wasn't part of the original plan. It only added to that feeling when the moment the door closed behind us, I heard Veronica's raised voice.

"This isn't how it was supposed to go, and you know it!"

"What do you mean 'not how it was supposed to go'?" Jeremy's voice yelled back. "Was I supposed to pander to that girl just because she's been here before?"

"You know that's not what I mean, you arrogant idiot!"

I let Neil and the other bakers slip ahead while I hung back to indulge my curiosity and eavesdrop on Jeremy and Veronica's argument. Not that it was difficult, given how loudly they were shouting. I probably could have heard them clearly even from the green room.

"What do I know?"

"*I'm* supposed to be the head judge! This is supposed to be my show!"

"Ha!" Jeremy scoffed loudly. "Your show? You can't carry a show! You have to have a face that moves for that!"

Veronica screamed so loudly and angrily that I jumped.

"Get her off me!" Jeremy shouted. Veronica kept screaming, sounding like an angry cat.

Several PAs rushed by, followed by Neil. He stopped when he saw me. "You should go wait in the green room, Fran. We'll come get you as soon as we're ready for the next shot."

I didn't want to go, but he stood there wearing a pained expression that I thought was intended to be a smile.

"Neil!" Gail's frantic voice managed to pierce Veronica's screams.

Neil's face was conflicted. I solved the problem for him by going to the green room. I glanced back over my shoulder as I stepped through the door and saw him running back to the set.

I was right that we could still hear the yelling from the green room, but it was muffled by Kaitlin, who was now full-out sobbing on Suzette's shoulder. I sat down on Kaitlin's other side and rubbed my hand in circles on her back.

"I won't work with her anymore!" Jeremy thundered as he passed our door, surrounded by a group of PAs.

"That's fine, because I'm not working with you, you pig!" Veronica shouted.

The shouting continued back and forth until we heard two doors slam.

We sat in perfect stillness, the sudden quiet broken only by Kaitlin's sobs, which had managed to intensify during the yelling. Gradually, even those faded to silence. Suzette looked down at Kaitlin, who had fallen asleep on her shoulder, then over at me. Together, we helped shift Kaitlin so she was lying down on the couch.

"I'm going to get a drink," Suzette said. I wasn't sure we were supposed to leave, but she wasn't bothered by that and walked out of the room. Later, Winston left, then Eduardo. After a while, I gave up and went for a bathroom and snack break too. Some of the PAs were gathered in a huddle, whispering near the craft services table.

"Do you guys know when we'll be filming again?" I asked them.

"I don't know. It'll probably be a while," one of them answered.

I went back to the green room and sat down. "It sounds like we'll be waiting a while," I told them.

Winston sighed and left the room again. Eduardo went out to make a phone call. Suzette wandered out and then back in again a while later. Eventually, Kaitlin woke up and rubbed her eyes. Between the sleeping and crying, she'd need to visit hair and makeup again before we could film anything else. I pulled out my phone to text Matt and see how the game was going.

Kaitlin jumped up suddenly. "I need to pee," she said and rushed from the room. At least she didn't throw up in the trash can again, which I noticed had been cleaned and replaced, or maybe just replaced. I wouldn't have blamed production if they'd chosen that option.

Suzette wandered back in a little while later. "Where's Kaitlin?" she asked.

"Bathroom break. She's actually been gone a while. Maybe I should go check on her."

Suzette nodded and sank into the couch.

I went down the hall and popped into the bathroom. It was completely empty. I passed a PA on my way out and stopped her. "Excuse me, is there another bathroom?"

Her eyes widened slightly as she glanced past me into the bathroom.

"Oh, no, there's nothing wrong with it—I just thought Kaitlin was in there, but she's not. I was wondering if she went to a different one."

The PA looked relieved. I wondered if one of her jobs was cleaning up the bathroom. I didn't envy her if it was. "There's another one by the set," she said and scooted past me.

I walked back to the green room and poked my head in to see if Kaitlin had returned. She hadn't, and now Eduardo was gone too. I didn't see either of them at craft services, so I continued down the hall, looking for at least Kaitlin. She really had been gone a while, and I was getting visions of her passed out in a heap in some deserted corner.

I paused for a moment to listen outside the rooms that had Jeremy Johnson's and Veronica Browning's names on the doors. Both were quiet. I moved on down the hall and turned a corner into another hallway.

I finally spotted Kaitlin standing in front of an open door, staring down at the floor.

I followed her gaze down to the floor and saw Jeremy Johnson lying there with a blue-handled knife in his chest.

Kaitlin screamed.

Chapter 14

I STARED in silence for a moment before coming to my senses. I turned and ran back the way I'd come. "Help! Help! We need help! We need the police!"

A PA came around the corner, looking annoyed.

"Call 911!" I shouted at him. "Jeremy Johnson's dead!" I saw the shock register in his eyes a split second before I realized I'd left Kaitlin back there with Jeremy's body and, for all I knew, a murderer nearby. I ran back down the hallway.

Kaitlin was still standing across from the open door, but she'd backed up against the opposite wall.

"Kaitlin!"

She looked at me.

I grabbed her arm and started pulling her away

from the body. "We can't be here. We have to preserve the evidence."

"Evidence?" She looked genuinely confused.

"For the police. We can't contaminate the crime scene."

Her forehead wrinkled, and she shook her head slightly. "Jeremy—"

"He's dead, Kaitlin. There's nothing we can do to help him." I hadn't touched his body or checked his pulse, but the gray pallor of his face and the unnatural stillness of his body had left no doubt in my mind.

She moaned and clutched her stomach, nearly doubling over. I had to practically drag her down the hall.

Two PAs rushed by us as we turned the corner. I heard their footsteps come to a sudden halt. "Oh my God," one said. She turned and ran back past us. "It's true! It's true! Call Gail! Get Neil! Somebody, call an ambulance!"

Kaitlin moaned again. I dragged her down the hallway toward the green room. She wasn't so much resisting as just not moving under her own power. It was almost as if she couldn't.

The other bakers were all standing in the

hallway or the green room doorway. "What's happening?" Eduardo asked.

"It's Jeremy Johnson. He—" I stopped and looked at Kaitlin then just shook my head. I wanted to get her lying down before she completely collapsed. "She needs to lie down."

Eduardo put an arm around Kaitlin and helped me half carry, half drag her across the room and lay her down on the couch. He took my elbow and guided me back to the door by Suzette and Winston. "What's happening, Fran?"

I took a deep, tremulous breath and realized for the first time how shaken up I was. "Jeremy—he—" I closed my eyes and took another breath. "He was stabbed. He was on the floor, and there was a knife —" I poked my fingers into the center of my chest.

Eduardo muttered something under his breath in Spanish. "You found him?"

I shook my head. "No, Kaitlin did." As soon as the words passed my lips, I saw the scene again in my mind—Kaitlin looking down at the ground, me looking at her then at Jeremy's body. Then Kaitlin's scream. How long had she been there before I walked up? Had she seen me before she screamed? *Why* had she been in that back hallway to begin with? It was nowhere near the bathroom or craft services or the green room. It was nowhere near anywhere she had a reason to be. Unless—I looked over my shoulder at her lying on the couch. She looked so innocent.

I turned back to the other bakers. "I think she's in shock."

Eduardo nodded as a troop of paramedics and police officers walked past us.

"We should have the paramedics check her," Suzette said. "Make sure she and the—" She hesitated. "Make sure she's okay."

I nodded and looked over at Kaitlin again. She was curled on her side, hands on her belly. I looked back at Suzette. She met my eyes and raised one eyebrow slightly.

I looked at her for a moment, wondering if she meant what I thought she did. I turned to Winston and Eduardo. "Can you guys wait out here and catch the paramedics when they come back through?" They both nodded, and I looked at Suzette, tipping my head to ask her to come wait in the room with me.

The two of us stepped into the room, far enough away from both the couch and the door that we wouldn't be overheard if we spoke softly. "Is she—do you think—?" I cut myself off, not wanting to say out loud what I thought Suzette was telling me in case I was wrong.

But Suzette nodded. "She's nauseous, tired, running to the bathroom all the time. Just like me when I was pregnant with my son."

I looked at Kaitlin again, and suddenly, I could see it. Her hands weren't on just any part of her belly but on the lower part that would swell first with a baby. The fatigue, the nausea—it all made sense. Even her tears when Jeremy and Veronica had criticized her cake. Though it made sense, given how harsh their criticism was, it made even more sense when I realized that she was dealing with pregnancy hormones too.

"How far along do you think she is?"

Suzette shrugged. "Three months, maybe four. If you look closely, she's not showing yet, but her clothes are beginning to get a little tight. She almost always unbuttons the top button of her pants when she sits down."

Suzette seemed so distant and aloof that I was surprised she'd noticed anything about Kaitlin, let alone such a small detail. "How did you notice that?"

Another shrug. "I had a feeling, so I watched."

I looked at Kaitlin. Her hands at her belly had

pulled her shirt up just enough that I could see the waistband of her pants. Sure enough, the top button was undone. I looked back at Suzette. "How old is your son?"

She smiled—the first time I'd seen a genuine look of happiness on her face. "He's fifteen."

"Fifteen? Wow! I wouldn't have guessed you're old enough to have a fifteen-year-old!"

"I was young. Too young. And naïve." She nodded toward Kaitlin. "She reminds me of myself at that age. My hair was even blond." She wrapped a curl around her finger, looking wistfully at Kaitlin or maybe thinking of herself back then. She exhaled sharply. "She'll be all right, though."

"Someone need the paramedics?" A woman in a tan button-down and brown cargo pants came in toting a duffel bag.

"She does." I gestured at Kaitlin.

"What's going on?" the paramedic asked in a gentle tone, squatting next to Kaitlin. Kaitlin had her eyes squeezed shut tight. I didn't think she was asleep, but I didn't think she was going to answer either.

"She found—the body," I said.

The paramedic nodded in understanding. "Any medical conditions?"

I hesitated, not wanting to share something I didn't know for sure. Suzette, though, motioned her hand in a curve over her belly.

The paramedic nodded. "If you'll give us some privacy…"

Suzette and I went out into the hall, and I pulled the door closed behind us. Suzette stood close beside Winston. His hand brushed hers as they whispered to each other. I leaned against the wall and heaved a heavy sigh. All I wanted was to fall into Matt's arms, but I was stuck in this studio while he was off watching baseball with his friend. I would have settled for at least hearing his voice, but my phone was in the green room.

Eduardo came and stood beside me. "Kaitlin is all right?"

I nodded. "I think so. The paramedic is checking her out."

"And you are all right?"

I tried to take a deep breath as I nodded, but the air caught in my throat in a surprising sob.

"You aren't. Of course you're not. No woman would be all right after finding a dead body."

I looked at him out of the corner of my eye. "I don't think it has anything to do with being a woman. It has to do with finding a man I spoke to three hours ago lying on the ground with a knife sticking out of his chest."

He inclined his head toward me with a chastised look. "Fair point."

I swallowed my feelings with another deep breath. Eduardo had the decency to back off and leave me alone.

Two suited detectives walked by with an understandably stressed-looking PA. One detective glared at each of us with narrowed eyes. The other seemed to completely ignore us in some odd variation of a stereotypical good-cop-slash-bad-cop duo—critical cop and oblivious cop.

Several more minutes passed before the green room door opened and the paramedic stepped out. She scanned our little group before settling her eyes on me. "She'll be fine. But she could use a friend."

I wasn't sure I was that, but I nodded and took the paramedic's place in the green room. Suzette followed me in.

Kaitlin was doubled over on the couch, weeping softly. Suzette and I sat down on either side of her. I placed my hand gently on Kaitlin's back.

She rocked as she cried. Like this, she seemed even younger than she was. I thought about what Suzette had said about being young and naïve.

"What am I going to do?" Kaitlin's voice was barely audible. "I never meant for this to happen."

Suzette and I exchanged a look over Kaitlin's head. I took a deep breath. I was afraid to ask, but I had to. "You never meant for what to happen, Kaitlin?"

"This!" She gestured at her body. "All of this!" A wave at the general room. She shook her head. "I grew up with a single mom. I never wanted to *be* one!"

Chapter 15

SUZETTE'S LIPS WERE TIGHT, and her eyes were cold.

I rubbed my hand in a big circle on Kaitlin's back, realizing she'd basically acknowledged the pregnancy. "I grew up with a single mom too. It's not so bad. You and your baby will have an extra-special bond when it's just the two of you."

"But it wasn't supposed to happen! I wasn't going to be!"

Suzette stood up abruptly and headed for the door. She jerked it open and was met by the two detectives we'd seen earlier.

"Are you the one who found the body?" It was the critical one.

Suzette's spine straightened ever so slightly, and

I thought she was going to shut the door in their faces. Instead, she stepped aside, gesturing into the room. "She's on the couch."

"Can I stay with her?" I asked.

"And you are?" The critical detective looked at me critically. The oblivious one behind him seemed to be examining the paint on the walls.

"My name is Francesca Amaro. I'm a friend."

"And you're here for what? Moral support?"

I bit the inside of my cheek. "Yes. Also, I'm the one who called for help, so I assume you'll want to talk to me too."

He smirked. "Oh, we will. But later. Leave us, and shut the door on your way out."

I looked at Kaitlin. *Young and naïve* echoed in my head.

"Now."

I leaned toward Kaitlin. "I'll be right outside the door. We all will."

She nodded ever so slightly.

Reluctantly, I got up and walked out into the hallway with Suzette. "Suzette."

She raised an eyebrow at me.

"I just—I don't think she meant to insult you."

She looked at me curiously.

"The single-mom comment." I realized

suddenly that she'd never actually said that. I'd just assumed based on the way she talked about her son. "You are one, aren't you? A single mom?"

She shook her head then hesitated. "I'm not, no. But I was one back when Jackson was born. I have a partner now, and my son has a man who actually wants to act like a father." She looked down at her clenched hands then back up at me. "She wasn't being unkind. Just grieving."

I wanted to ask what she meant, but not here, not now. Not in front of Winston and Eduardo. I took the same spot I'd had before, leaning against the wall. I reached for my pocket to text Matt then sighed in annoyance when I realized my phone was still in the green room.

A uniformed police officer came down the hall from the direction where Jeremy Johnson's body lay. She knocked twice, hard and fast, on the green room door. The critical detective opened it. "The Crime Scene Response Unit is ready for you, sir."

He nodded sharply. "Tell them we'll be right there. And get this group into separate rooms where they can't work on their story."

"Yes, sir."

The door snapped closed. The officer looked at the group of us. "Uh, follow me, I guess."

She started down the hall away from the body. We dutifully fell in behind her. She stopped in craft services and looked around uneasily until a PA wandered through. "Excuse me, are there rooms I can put these people in?"

"Um, the green room?" The PA looked unfazed by the murder investigation going on around him and simultaneously like he thought she must be stupid to ask where the contestants went when we obviously had a place where we belonged.

She looked back at us. Eduardo shook his head. "That is where we came from."

"Somewhere else," the officer said to the PA, feigning confidence. I wondered how long she'd been on the job. "They need to be separated."

The PA rolled his eyes. "I guess you could spread them out in here. We don't exactly have holding cells or anything."

A chill went down my spine at the mention of holding cells. We couldn't possibly be suspects in the murder, could we? We'd all just met Jeremy that day —except Kaitlin. She'd received the harshest critique too. I shook the thought off and focused my attention on the poor officer trying to figure out what to do with the four of us that wouldn't get her in trouble with the detectives.

She squared her shoulders and pointed to the folding chairs around the tables in the middle. "We'll spread those chairs out around the room. That should be enough separation." She looked over her shoulder as she headed that way. "If you could help me, please?"

The PA rolled his eyes again but followed her. He grabbed a chair and dragged it across the room, seeming to make as much noise as possible. Eduardo rushed over. "I'll help you, Officer, uh—" He looked at the name tag pinned to her chest. "Officer Murphy." He grinned, flashing his exceptionally white teeth. I thought I saw the officer blush.

Eduardo picked up a chair. "Where would you like it?"

"Over in the corner, please." She grabbed another chair and toted it to the opposite corner. Neither of them made even a fraction of the racket the PA had—the PA who, notably, scampered away as soon as he dropped off his chair.

Eduardo and Officer Murphy made it back to the last chair at the same time. He flashed his grin again and picked it up before she could, carrying it off across the room. He dropped it off and returned to our group.

Officer Murphy thanked him and smiled apologetically. "Now I need you all to take a seat in one of the chairs. No talking about the case—or anything. I have to go talk to CSRU—the crime scene team—and then I'll be back."

"If there's anything else I can do for you, I'd be happy to be of service." Eduardo looked at her as if he wasn't necessarily talking about hauling chairs around.

She definitely blushed this time. "Thank you, uh—"

"Eduardo."

"Eduardo."

For a second, I thought he was going to take her hand and kiss it, but he just smiled and sauntered off to the last chair he'd put out and fixed his sultry gaze on her. The rest of us followed his lead—minus the sultry gaze—and took chairs around the room. Officer Murphy left us to go do whatever she needed to. We actually behaved and didn't talk to each other.

After a long while, Kaitlin walked in. She looked at us spread around the room then sat down in one of the chairs still at the table and put her head in her hands. She looked like she'd been through the wringer. Her hair was messy, and more of her mascara was under her eyes than on them. Slowly, she put her head down on the table.

Officer Murphy rejoined us and took a place against the wall where she could see all of us. Her eyes occasionally swept the room. Every time they landed on Eduardo, she had to fight back a smile. He didn't bother trying to hide it—just grinned at her.

It felt like we sat there for an eternity as Eduardo flirted with the officer, Kaitlin rested with her head on the table, and Winston scrolled on his phone. Suzette seemed distinctly unworried by our wait. She sat calmly with her eyes closed and her hands resting on her lap. I was pretty sure she was meditating.

I was still annoyed that I'd left my phone in the green room. I wondered if Matt had noticed he hadn't heard from me. I hoped he wasn't worrying. Of course, I'd warned him that the filming might keep me busy, so maybe he assumed that's what I was doing. What would he think when he found out I'd somehow managed to get myself involved in yet *another* murder? It had happened far too many times since I'd returned to Cape Bay.

Eventually, there was a commotion down the hall. I sat up and craned my neck to see what was going on but then wished I hadn't. The paramedics were wheeling a stretcher down the hall, and I could only assume that the contents of the body bag on top were Jeremy Johnson's earthly remains. Not that there was any doubt, but the tent shape where the bag had been zipped over the knife in his chest gave it away.

The two detectives followed the stretcher outside then came back. They conferred briefly with each other before the oblivious one—who still hadn't even seemed to glance at any of us—headed down the hallway toward the green room.

"Everything okay here, Officer?" the critical one asked Officer Murphy.

She straightened up. "Yes, sir. All quiet."

He nodded brusquely. He pulled a notebook out of his suit pocket, turned a few pages, then flipped it closed. "Is one of you Francesca Amaro?"

I put my hand up.

"Come with me, please. We have a few questions for you."

Chapter 16

"ALL RIGHT, Francesca, I'm Detective Mulholland. Could you state your full name and address for me?"

The critical detective—Detective Mulholland— had led me back to the green room. I restrained myself from going straight for my phone but only barely. Detective Mulholland instructed me to sit on the couch. He took an armchair he'd apparently relocated to the middle of the room. The oblivious detective, still nameless, was already seated on the far side of the room with his elbow propped on the end table, fiddling with a rubber band.

"Francesca Antonia Amaro, 231 Bay Street, Cape Bay, Massachusetts."

The oblivious detective's head snapped up. "Cape Bay?"

I nodded.

"You know Mike Stanton, by any chance?"

I nodded again.

"Does he know you?"

I smiled. "Yes, he does. We grew up together. And he comes into my café pretty much every day."

That was actually an understatement. Mike came in at least once a day to get a black coffee that he drank scalding hot. I didn't know how he did it —it was painful just to watch. I also chose not to mention that I had helped Mike solve more than one murder case recently. Well, "helped solve" might not be the words Mike would choose. "Interfered with" would probably be how he described it.

Detective Mulholland waited to see if Oblivious Detective had anything else to say, but he had already gone back to staring blankly at the carpet and playing with his rubber band. Now I knew he wasn't completely oblivious. Some part of him was listening at least a little.

"Okay, Francesca, how about you tell us what happened today?"

I didn't like the look on Detective Mulholland's face. It seemed somehow accusatory, like he suspected me of being involved in more than just calling for help. I set my jaw and told him what had happened—the long delay, being worried about Kaitlin, going to look for her, finding Jeremy Johnson's body. I didn't volunteer how critical he'd been of Kaitlin or that I'd heard him and Veronica Browning arguing. I wasn't sure why I didn't share those details—maybe it felt too much like I was pointing fingers, maybe I was afraid to point the detectives at someone I liked, or maybe I just didn't like the look on Detective Mulholland's face. Whatever the reason, I left that information out, even though I knew that had Mike Stanton been the detective on the case, he would have been furious with me for it. Come to think of it, maybe that was the reason I was leaving it out—these detectives weren't Mike, and I didn't know them like I knew him. I trusted Mike to be fair, but Critical and Oblivious here were unknown quantities. I wasn't willing to point the finger at someone potentially innocent when I wasn't sure that they were going to do their jobs properly.

"Anything else you want to tell us?" Mulholland asked.

For a second, I thought he knew I hadn't been completely forthcoming, but then I realized that it was probably just a standard question. I thought for a moment about whether there actually *was* anything else I wanted to tell them then shook my head. "Not that I can think of."

Mulholland sighed, looking annoyed that I hadn't handed him his case on a silver platter covered in the murderer's fingerprints. "Go back to the lunchroom and wait. Don't talk to anyone."

I stood up and made it halfway to the door before I remembered my phone. Matt had to be wondering where I was by now. "Oh, can I just grab my phone?" I started over to the little cubbies where we'd stashed our bags.

"No!" Mulholland spoke so sharply that I jumped. "We don't need you contacting the media."

"But Winst—"

"Back to the lunchroom, Ms. Amaro, before I think there's something on that phone you want to hide from me."

I left the room without looking at either of them. My cheeks burned with embarrassment. I was glad I hadn't told them anything but the basic facts. They couldn't expect more—they didn't *deserve* more—when they spoke to people like that.

Back in craft services, I stared at my shoes and tried to take deep breaths to calm down. Eventually,

I noticed Eduardo trying to catch my eye. I looked up at him, and he formed the 'okay' symbol with his fingers while giving a questioning look. Tears burned my eyes, and I looked back at the floor. They'd made me feel like a criminal, when I'd been the one to call for help. Who knew how long Kaitlin would have—or had—stood there staring if I hadn't walked up?

I glanced up as Mulholland came back into the room. He smirked at me. I wanted to glare back but didn't want to antagonize him just in case his comment about my phone had been more serious than grandstanding.

"Suzette Collins?"

Suzette stood up regally and crossed the room to the detective. I wondered if Mulholland noticed Winston still scrolling on his phone or if he was too focused on his next interview to pay attention. I gritted my teeth as Suzette followed the detective back down the hall.

It seemed like an eternity before Suzette came back and Mulholland returned for Eduardo. Police officers came and went, Kaitlin napped, Winston scrolled on his phone, and I resorted to counting the various pieces of equipment that hung over our heads in place of a ceiling. For the record: fourteen beams, five air ducts, eighty-seven wires or wirelike things, and eleven pieces of some kind of metal with twenty-four holes in each of the seven sections that I could see on each piece. I counted twice to be sure.

Eduardo returned, Mulholland took Winston to the back, and I started studying the smudges and stains on the concrete floor, looking for some sort of pattern that might be vaguely interesting. There wasn't one.

Winston came back, and we sat for a while longer. I wondered what time it was. It felt as if hours had passed, but it could have been forty-five minutes for all I knew. There was no clock anywhere that I could see. I rubbed my wrist, wishing for a watch even though I knew the production crew probably wouldn't have let me wear it and I would have taken it off and left it with my phone in the stupid green room that I was banned from.

I heaved a frustrated sigh and roughly adjusted my position in my chair. The chair scraped across the concrete floor, making everyone turn and look at me. I forced what I hoped was an apologetic smile and almost immediately went back to scowling at the wall. Sitting still for long periods of time with nothing to do wasn't one of my strong points. Especially when I didn't have so much as a scrap of paper to scribble on.

Kaitlin sat up and looked around the room in confusion. "How long have I been asleep?"

"No talking, please." Officer Murphy's voice was less than authoritative and had no effect on Winston, the only one of us who seemed to know. "Three hours and seventeen minutes," he said.

"Are you serious?" I blurted before I could think twice.

"Guys, please—" Officer Murphy looked around at us anxiously.

Winston rolled his bespectacled eyes in my direction. "All too serious."

"I need to eat something." Kaitlin glanced around, looking mildly nauseous. Her eyes landed on the craft services table, and she started to stand up. Remembering what had happened earlier and not thinking at all about having been told to stay in our chairs, I jumped up and ran to grab her some snacks.

"You should all be—" Officer Murphy started.

"She's pregnant!" I shouted as I hurled myself toward the craft services table on stiff legs. I grabbed a bowl of fruit and plate of crackers, practically throwing them at Kaitlin. She sank back down in her chair and smiled at me appreciatively. I'd started to move back toward the uncomfortable metal folding chair I'd passed the last few hours in when I realized Officer Murphy hadn't moved from her spot by the wall. I stopped and stretched, reaching my arms over my head and arching my back. After a couple of pops from my joints, I walked back to my chair, but the damage had been done.

Winston was the first to stand up. He stretched his long body in a smooth series of athletic moves and looked like he was about to run a race.

Suzette was next, standing gracefully and moving through a series of quick yoga moves. Then Eduardo stood. He didn't stretch as much as the rest of us but rolled back and forth on the balls of his feet. Kaitlin alone stayed seated as she downed her crackers and fruit. Officer Murphy stood by the wall, looking panicked at our disobedience but also uneasy about whether she should intervene. We were all where we were supposed to be but not doing what we were supposed to be doing.

That was, of course, the moment Detective Mulholland walked into the room.

His eyes widened as he looked around at all of us, standing, stretching, looking like we were about to get up to who knows what in his mind. He looked at Officer Murphy. Her pale skin flamed red. "Care to explain, Officer?"

"I—um—uh," she stammered, looking terrified.

"A stretch break!" I blurted.

She looked at me, and I nodded quickly, encouraging her to go with it.

She exhaled visibly. "Thank you, Ms. Amaro." She turned to the detective. "I offered them a moment to stand up and stretch their legs since they'd been sitting for so long. Like we learned in training, sir, sitting too long can cause blood clots. I didn't want anyone to have any complications on our watch."

Mulholland almost looked as if he believed her.

"And this one"—she nodded at Kaitlin—"she's expecting, sir. We wouldn't want to be on the hook for anything going wrong with that."

His eyes narrowed, but eventually, he nodded. "You'll all be taken back to your hotel momentarily. Do not go anywhere without explicit permission from me or one of the other detectives on the case. Do not leave the hotel, do not leave the city, do not leave the state. Do not leave the country." He looked pointedly at Eduardo with that last part.

Eduardo put his hands up defensively. "I'm

from Texas," he said, his accent suddenly not quite as thick as it had been. He looked at the rest of us, shrugged, and smiled. "Gail said playing up my accent made for better TV. Who am I to argue?"

"Whatever," Mulholland snapped. "Just nobody go anywhere. And don't talk about the case. To anyone." He glared at each of us in turn. "Someone will be here to drive you to the hotel shortly."

"I'll believe that when I see it," Winston muttered, sitting back down in his chair and pulling his phone back out.

Mulholland had turned to go, but he spun back around on his heel and stared at Winston. "What did you say?"

Winston looked at him coolly. "You heard me."

For a moment, I thought Mulholland was going to explode at Winston, but the oblivious detective chose that moment to obliviously step into the room. He shoved his hands into the pockets of his suit pants and cleared his throat.

Mulholland glanced over his shoulder at Detective Oblivious and then, with a final scowl at Winston, turned to leave.

"Um, Detective?" I called, tempting fate. He turned his scowl toward me.

"Can I get my phone from the green room before we go? Please?"

His scowl found a way to deepen. "No. Everything that's here stays here." With that, he left.

Oblivious whispered something to Officer Murphy, who nodded and said, "Yes, sir." Then Oblivious followed Mulholland out of the room.

When their footsteps had faded away, Officer Murphy glanced down the hall after them then took a deep breath. "Someone from the TV crew will be here to take you back to the hotel in a few minutes."

"When will we be able to resume filming?" Suzette asked.

My head snapped in her direction. Were we going to continue filming? It hadn't even occurred to me. Of course, it hadn't occurred to me that we wouldn't either. I hadn't thought about it at all either way.

"That's a question for the detectives," Officer Murphy said. "And your TV people, of course."

I looked at my fellow bakers to gauge their reactions to Suzette's question. I couldn't imagine we'd be continuing, but was I alone in that?

Eduardo was the only one whose eye I managed to catch. He shrugged before his eyes flitted back to Officer Murphy. She kept looking his direction too.

I sat down to wait.

It was only a few minutes before Neil came in. "I'm driving you back to the hotel. Is everyone ready?" He started for the door without waiting for a response or to make sure we were following.

"I have to pee," Kaitlin said.

Neil glanced down the hall toward the only bathrooms and then at Officer Murphy. She shook her head. Neil waved toward the door. "We'll stop at a McDonald's or something if you can't hold it until we get to the hotel."

I had a sudden flashback to my mother saying nearly the same thing to me when I was a child and we were leaving for a road trip.

I tried to linger toward the back of the group, wondering if I could sneak off down the hallway to grab my phone and purse. It was probably a terrible idea, but… there was no chance anyway. Our group was too small, and Neil was moving too quickly.

Eduardo managed to hang back long enough to stop and talk to Officer Murphy, who blushed as red as ever when he touched her hand ever so briefly before darting up to join us.

"What was that about?" I asked.

He winked. "A gentleman never tells."

In the van, we sat quietly, a combination of exhaustion and obedience to the detective's orders. Kaitlin managed to hold her bladder until we got to the hotel, but only just. She practically leapt from the van and ran into the lobby bathroom. I trudged up to my room, only realizing after I got there that my room key was in my purse, which was locked in the green room back at the studio. And I had no way of contacting Matt to see if he was even nearby.

I rested my head against the door and gave a couple of hopeful knocks. I doubted Matt was inside—he'd seemed to be having a great time with his buddy and without me—but the prospect of going all the way back to the lobby to try to convince the front desk to give me a new key card with no ID or proof that I was staying there was daunting. It had been such a long day.

I almost fell as the door opened. "Franny! You lose your key?"

I grasped Matt, letting him wrap me in his arms. I nestled my head into his chest, wanting to forget for just a moment the rollercoaster of the day and the past few weeks. For just tonight, I wanted to forget every doubt I'd had recently and take comfort in Matt's presence.

"What's wrong, babe? You didn't get eliminated, did you?"

I shook my head without looking up.

He put his hands on my shoulders and took a half step back. "Franny?"

Before I could say anything, there was a knock at the door.

Matt stepped around me and opened it. My stomach dropped as I saw Detective Oblivious over his shoulder.

"Hi, I'm Sergeant Coburn with the BPD. May I come in?"

Chapter 17

SERGEANT COBURN STUDIED me from across the room. He sat in the desk chair, while I perched on the edge of the bed next to Matt. Coburn had been reluctant to let Matt stay, but I'd insisted that I'd be more comfortable with him there, and Coburn had eventually relented. Now we sat, staring at each other in the silence I'd grown to expect from my encounters with him. The only thing I'd heard him ask before he showed up in my hotel room was if I knew Mike, and even that had been an incredibly brief exchange.

I fidgeted next to Matt. It had occurred to me that he had no idea the set of *Hometown Showdown* had been a murder scene today, and now there was a Boston police detective sitting in our hotel room.

Matt was taking it remarkably in stride. I wasn't sure if that was a good sign or a bad one for our relationship.

"So, Sergeant, what can we help you with?" Matt asked.

Coburn ignored him, studying his notebook. His lips pursed as he drummed his pen on it. Then his eyes focused on mine. "I gave Mike Stanton a call."

My mouth went dry.

"You know Mike?" Matt asked amiably.

I elbowed him in the side. There was no reason to think that Mike would have told this detective anything bad about me—at least, not on purpose. I could see how my tendency to get involved with murder investigations wasn't necessarily something another detective might consider "good," though. Especially not a detective in a big city like Boston. Tiny Cape Bay was practically a different world.

Coburn ignored Matt's question and continued to stare at me. "What do you think he told me about you?"

I swallowed hard. "Good things, I hope."

He raised an eyebrow. Then a corner of his mouth turned up. "Very good things, in fact." He paused. "Well, if you consider 'a giant pain in the butt' to be a good thing."

Somehow, I thought that Mike's choice of words had probably been a little more colorful than Sergeant Coburn's interpretation of them, but otherwise, I couldn't claim to be surprised that that was how he'd described me. But whether it was a good thing, I had no idea.

"He also said I'd be a fool not to take advantage of you being so closely involved."

Well, that was for sure a good thing.

"Involved? Involved in what?" Matt asked.

I was beginning to regret talking Coburn into letting him stay.

Coburn raised an eyebrow. "You haven't told him?"

I glanced at Matt and shook my head. "I didn't get a chance. I walked in right before you got here."

Coburn nodded then looked at Matt. "Jeremy Johnson was murdered on set today."

"What?" Matt leapt up then immediately knelt in front of me and took my hands. "Are you okay, Franny? Were you there? Did you see anything?"

A rush of emotion flooded over me. The day had been long and challenging and emotional, and even though I'd spent all that time sitting in craft services, waiting to be released, I hadn't actually thought about the horrors of what I'd seen and what had happened. I fought back tears as the image of Jeremy Johnson's body on the floor floated in front of my eyes.

"Franny, oh, Franny." Matt pulled me against him and stroked my back.

"I'll give you a minute." Coburn stood up and went to the door, flipping the swing bar so he could open the door again from outside. And probably to hear anything Matt and I said.

I cried into Matt's neck.

"Shh, babe, it's okay. I'm here."

It hadn't just been a long day—it had been a long few *weeks* with Matt acting weird and then the show and then Matt still acting weird and then the murder. I fought to get myself under control. If I really let go, I was afraid I'd be a sobbing mess for the rest of the day or maybe longer. I just couldn't face it all, not right now. Not with a homicide detective standing outside the door.

I took deep breaths, trying to calm down. Slowly, I managed to get myself together. Matt moved up to sit beside me on the bed again, rubbing my back and holding me close.

One last shaky breath, and I sat up straight, channeling my mother's and grandmother's words whenever they'd coached me through emotional times. "I'm okay. I'm okay," I repeated, as much to Matt as to myself. I stood up. "I'm going to go splash some water on my face, and then I'll be okay," I said loudly enough for Coburn to hear in the hallway and also partly to try to convince myself.

In the bathroom, I ran the cold water and looked at myself in the mirror. I was a wreck—my hair falling down, my not-so-waterproof mascara puddled under my puffy eyes. I wasn't sure a splash of water would do much for my appearance, but it would at least help my mental state.

I wet down a washcloth and pressed it onto my face. I used a corner to make an attempt at the mascara rings, but it seemed the mascara was more resistant to cold water than to tears. I tried to take my hair down, but it had been sprayed to within an inch of its life, so I ended up just running the washcloth over it in an attempt to smooth it down a little. When I was done, I didn't look good or even presentable, but it was moderately better than before.

I pulled open the door. Coburn was standing off

to the side at a discreet distance but still obviously within earshot. "I'm ready."

He followed me back into the room, where we resumed our seats. Matt sat closer this time, with his arm around me. His expression said he wouldn't hesitate to kick Coburn out if he made me cry again. Not that it was Coburn's fault that I'd burst into tears. Except that maybe it was. In any case, he at least had the decency to look vaguely remorseful.

"As I was saying, uh, before—" He waved his hand. "I gave Mike Stanton a call—"

"And he said I'm a pain in the butt." For some reason, I was trying to put Coburn at ease even though he was the one who had invited himself into my hotel room. Too many years in hospitality, probably.

To my surprise, Coburn grinned. "He did say that. And that you have good instincts that I'd be a fool not to take advantage of." He looked at me, gauging my reaction for a moment before continuing. "Obviously, we're very early in our investigation. And high-profile cases like this one are complicated, especially given the victim's—" He paused again, searching for the right word. "Reputation. We have no reason to suspect that any of your fellow contestants was involved with Mr. Johnson's death—beyond Ms. Winslow finding the body, of course—but one of you might have seen something without even realizing what you saw."

He was clearly leading up to something, but I didn't know what yet. Did he think I was hiding something? Had he somehow found out that Kaitlin hadn't screamed until *after* she saw me?

Coburn leaned forward, folded his hands, and rested his elbows on his knees. "Fran, I want you to talk to the other contestants for me. Listen to them. I'm not asking you to rat anyone out or snitch, and I definitely don't want you to do anything dangerous. I just want you to watch—and listen. And if there's anything you think I should know, anything that will help us bring Mr. Johnson's killer to justice, then you can tell me. Does that sound like something you can do?"

I nodded hesitantly. "Detective Mulholland said—"

"I outrank Mulholland. He's young and new to homicide. He's still learning how not to be a—he's still learning that vinegar doesn't catch many flies. Anyway, I'm the senior detective on this case, so what I say goes as far as how we handle the investigation."

Suddenly, I understood their dynamic. Mulholland might have been critical, but Coburn wasn't oblivious at all. He was watching. Listening. Acting like he wasn't paying attention so we would eventually let our guard down and tell him what he wanted to know.

I'd had a boss like that once. She would let us argue things out for an entire meeting until, two minutes before we were scheduled to adjourn and no closer to a solution than we'd been at the start, she'd casually state the solution to our problem as if it was the most obvious thing in the world. She spent whole meetings listening to our arguments and mentally processing them without saying a word until the end. I had loved working for her.

I thought for a moment then nodded. "Okay. I'm in."

Coburn leaned back in the chair, a faint smile crossing his face.

"How do you want me to do it, though? We're not supposed to talk about the case. I don't think we're even supposed to leave our rooms."

He waved his hand. "Nobody ever listens to us when we tell them not to talk about it. We'll get you all in the same room, and people will start talking." He stood up and took a step toward the door. Matt and I stood to follow him. "I don't expect anything to come of this. There's no motive. You all just met Johnson today, right?"

"Except Kaitlin," I said before I realized what I was doing.

Coburn just nodded. "Right. She was on another one of these last year. Still, I'd be surprised." He walked to the door, Matt and I trailing behind.

"How do I contact you? If I do find out anything? I don't have my phone."

"Almost forgot." Coburn reached into his pocket, brought out my cell phone, and held it out to me. "Like I said, Mulholland needs to learn when to use honey."

As the door closed behind him, I looked down at the phone to see what I'd missed during the day. There were a few messages from Sammy, updating me on minor events from the café, and one from Rhonda, making a joke. But despite me being out of touch for almost twelve hours, there were absolutely none from Matt.

Chapter 18

AFTER COBURN LEFT, I got into the shower, telling Matt that I needed to get all the makeup and hairspray off before I could do anything else. It wasn't a lie, but I also needed some time to think. And possibly cry. I wasn't ruling that out.

It took three shampoos before my hair started to feel even vaguely normal. I finally stopped washing it, not because all the hairspray was out but because I was tired of scrubbing. *At least it will be the hair and makeup people's problem to deal with*, I thought before remembering that I didn't actually know if we'd be continuing filming at all.

I turned the shower water so hot it was almost painful, hoping to distract myself from the pain in my heart. I didn't want to think about *Hometown*

Showdown or Jeremy Johnson or even Matt at the moment, to be honest. I just wanted everything to be normal. I wanted my mother back.

I let the tears roll down my face and the water muffle my sobs for a while before finally turning the shower off. I was exhausted and wanted nothing more than to fall into bed and sleep until morning or afternoon or Jeremy Johnson's murder was solved and I could go home.

But no such luck.

"Somebody from the TV crew came to the door while you were in the shower. You have dinner downstairs in"—Matt looked at the clock on his phone—"twenty minutes, now."

I sighed and sat down on the bed. I didn't know if I could do it. I'd promised Coburn, but what would—or could—he do to me if I just... didn't talk to the other bakers? I couldn't see him punishing me somehow for failing to find anything out when he himself had said he didn't expect anything to come of my mission.

Matt sat down next to me and put his arm around me. I rested my head on his shoulder. "Can you come with me?"

"I would, but I already have plans for this evening."

I sat up and tried to hide my disappointment.

"I'm meeting my buddy and his wife for dinner."

"Maybe I can ditch the group and go with you?"

An expression I didn't recognize crossed Matt's face. Fear?

"I wish you could, babe, but I don't think that Sergeant Coburn would be too happy about that."

I opened my mouth to protest, but Matt cut me off.

"Besides, the reservation is only for three."

A piece of my heart broke off. I stood up and went into the bathroom, closing the door and locking it behind me. Yet again, I fought off tears. I pressed my face into a towel until I got my breathing under control. Then I turned the blow dryer on, set my jaw, and went to work blowing out my hair. It was an endeavor any day, but it was even worse today with my hair still gunky with hair products. At least it gave me an excuse to hide in the bathroom. I kept the door locked.

I managed to get down to the hotel restaurant just a couple of minutes late. Even so, I was the last one to arrive.

I took the empty chair between Kaitlin and Eduardo. Suzette and Winston sat opposite us.

We exchanged neutral pleasantries, obviously on our guard to avoid the topic of Jeremy Johnson's murder as we'd been instructed. I wondered when —or if—Coburn's assurance that people would talk about it regardless would kick in.

We lasted until our food was delivered.

Winston had just picked up his fork when Eduardo raised a hand. "I suggest we have a moment of silence for Jeremy."

The rest of us looked at each other one by one. Finally, Winston put down his fork. We bowed our heads in silence. Kaitlin made a little gasping noise, and I reached over to take her hand.

After a few seconds, Eduardo called an end to our little tribute. "There is nothing our departed friend would like *less* than for us to let our food get cold!" He picked up his fork with gusto and dug into his food. The rest of us followed.

Except Kaitlin.

I leaned over to her. "You okay?"

She nodded, though I could see the tears in her eyes. "I just can't believe he's gone." She pressed a hand to her stomach.

I cocked my head, looking at her for a moment. *I wonder...*

Kaitlin looked at me, and I turned to my food. This wasn't the time.

"Did you all hear him arguing with Veronica Browning after judging?" Suzette asked. No need to specify who *he* was.

"How could we not? They were screaming at each other," I said.

"Did anyone tell the police about that?" Winston looked at each of us.

I looked at Eduardo and Kaitlin then shook my head. They did too. "I didn't want to seem like I was pointing fingers. What about you guys?"

Winston and Suzette glanced at each other then shook their heads. "I'm not a snitch," Winston said.

Did I see him looking toward me when he said it? Or was that my imagination? I usually had no qualms about helping the police—well, Mike—with an investigation, but this time, I felt different. Maybe because I felt a connection with my fellow bakers and didn't know Coburn from Adam. For all I knew, Coburn's first name might *be* Adam. He hadn't bothered to share that. No wonder I felt more allegiance to the bakers than to him.

"What will happen now? They'll probably send us home, no?" Eduardo asked.

Suzette stabbed a piece of lettuce from her salad. "I'm sure they have another judge they can bring in."

Kaitlin sniffled beside me. She'd barely touched her food. "I don't think I could do it. Going into that kitchen and him not being there——" She put her head in her hand and shook her head. "I couldn't do it."

"I don't see how we can continue," I said. "They already have the footage from today with him in it. They'd have to start over. But everyone will know this is the episode he died during. It would be terrible publicity for Baking Network to continue. I don't even know if they can keep going with the show at all after this. Maybe they can just drop this one if they already have a few other episodes in the can, but otherwise, they probably just need to drop the idea and take insurance money."

The other bakers looked at me.

I blushed. "I was in PR before I took over my family's café. I dealt with stuff like this all the time. Well, not *murder*, but——" I shut my mouth and focused on eating. I didn't need to discuss my history with murder with them. Especially if I had any thoughts of helping Coburn.

"So you think it was Veronica, then?" Eduardo asked after a few minutes of silent chewing.

I looked up to see who he was talking to. It was Winston or Suzette, but I couldn't tell which.

Winston shrugged. "Seems like the obvious suspect, doesn't it? With how they were yelling?"

"I think she attacked him too." Everyone turned to look at me. "I hung back a little. I heard him yell, 'Get her off me.' I could be wrong, though."

"You need to tell the police," Kaitlin said softly.

"I don't want to point fingers. I—" I realized everyone else was nodding in agreement with Kaitlin. "I'll tell them." At least that would be *something* to tell Coburn. "So, do *all* of you think it was Veronica?"

"I don't think it was her, but I don't think it *wasn't* her either," Winston said. "It could have been anybody. It could have been Kaitlin, for all I know. He ripped her a new one, and then she found the body. That's gotta look suspicious."

"What?" Kaitlin cried out. Her eyes filled with tears. "I didn't—I wouldn't—I couldn't—I—"

Suzette shot Winston an angry glance.

"He didn't mean it. He was just giving an example." I rubbed Kaitlin's back gently.

Suzette was still glaring at Winston.

"Yeah, it was an example. Any of us could have done it. We were all in and out of that room. And dude was a jerk. There were probably lots of people who wanted him dead."

"He's not known for being a nice guy—that's for sure."

Kaitlin's back was still shaking with each shuddering breath.

"Let's talk about something else." I was betraying my commission from Sergeant Coburn, but I couldn't take it anymore. Not with Kaitlin crying like this. I didn't know whether it was from the pregnancy or because she'd known him before or something else, but the slight possibility of helping the police wasn't worth making her cry.

The other bakers seemed to agree. There was a pause in our conversation as Kaitlin regained her composure and the rest of us focused on our food. Eduardo eventually broke the silence. "Fran, where's your boyfriend? I thought he'd be joining us."

"He had to go... somewhere... out... I mean, he couldn't come. He's not here." Now my eyes were the ones filling with tears as I struggled to put a sentence together.

"He just left you here?" Suzette asked. "After everything that happened today?"

I nodded. Kaitlin reached over and squeezed my hand. I felt pathetic.

There was a long, uncomfortable silence as everyone looked at me and Kaitlin with sorrowful expressions. I finally couldn't take it anymore and went with the New England failsafe. "So, how does everyone think the Patriots will do this year?"

To Matt's eternal dismay, I knew roughly nothing about sports except how to introduce them into a conversation to change the subject. Normally, being in the middle of a football conversation bored me to tears, but at the moment, I preferred it to being in tears for other reasons—like murder. Or my apparently failing relationship.

Matt hadn't yet returned when I got back to our room. I texted him to say that I was going to bed, waited as long as I could stand it, then texted again that I loved him and goodnight. I fell into a fitful sleep that didn't get any better when Matt finally came in.

"Franny?" he called softly.

I faced the wall and pretended I was asleep. His

breath smelled like beer as he kissed me on the cheek and whispered, "Love you," before settling down next to me. I pressed my face into the pillow and willed myself to fall asleep or, at the very least, not wake Matt with my tears.

Chapter 19

MATT WAS IN THE SHOWER, and I was lounging in bed the next morning when there was a knock at the door. I tried to ignore it, wanting to pretend the day before hadn't happened and wondering if I could sneak out of the hotel and back to Cape Bay, but they knocked again. Whoever it was wasn't going to leave me alone.

I dragged myself out of bed and checked the peephole. It was one of the PAs I'd seen wandering around the set yesterday.

I opened the door and looked at him.

"Van back to set leaves in half an hour. Please be on time." He walked away without saying anything else.

I sighed and shut the door. So much for sneaking out.

"Are you going to be done soon?" I asked, poking my head into the bathroom. I wanted to take a few minutes to let some scalding hot water pour over me, but I also needed to get dressed and grab something for breakfast. Of course, I could always take my chances that the craft services table would be stocked. Although, would it be if we weren't filming? *Were* we filming? I had no idea. The PA hadn't bothered to share any of that.

"I'll be a couple more minutes." Matt stuck his head out of the curtain with a mischievous grin. "Unless you want to join me?"

Well, I certainly didn't have time for *that*. "Apparently, I have to go back to the set, so no, not today."

"Next time." He winked and ducked back into the shower.

I brushed my teeth, put on a bare minimum of makeup, threw some clothes on, and hoped I was appropriately dressed for whatever we would be doing.

"I'm going to go down to try to grab some breakfast real quick," I called to Matt, who was still in the shower—he took the longest showers of anyone I'd ever met, man or woman.

"'Kay. Love you." Matt poked his head out again. "How long do you think you'll be?"

A surge of hope that he wanted to hang out with me flared. "I'm not sure—the guy didn't say. I can let you know as soon as I find out, though."

"Great. The Sox have another day game today, and I'd love to hit it up if we can. Chris's boss is a big fan, so he doesn't mind him skipping out on work to catch a game."

Thrown over for the Boston Red Sox again. Matt had spent more time watching baseball the past few days than he had with me. I knew I couldn't be too upset since I'd been working the whole time, and Matt was just tagging along to keep me company, but it still hurt, and not just because I'd had a fleeting thought that he wanted to go to the game with *me*. I probably wouldn't have enjoyed it, but it would have been nice to be asked.

I bit back my disappointment. "I'll let you know as soon as I do." I blew him a kiss to avoid getting wet and headed downstairs in hopes of catching the breakfast buffet before they shut it down or the van left.

I had just enough time to grab a plate of eggs

and a cup of bad hotel coffee and scarf them down before the other bakers started to gather by the door. I grabbed one of the mini boxes of cereal in case Kaitlin needed something and went to join them.

"Good morning! How is everyone on this beautiful day?" Eduardo asked when he joined us. He was the most stubbornly upbeat and social of our group.

I looked around to find us all—except Eduardo —looking a little the worse for wear, Kaitlin in particular. Her eyes were puffy and red with dark circles beneath them. Her blond hair looked like it hadn't seen a brush or probably a shower. I felt bad that I hadn't thought to check on her after dinner last night. It was probably a rough night all alone in her hotel room.

Suzette, for her part, looked like she hadn't slept well. She wore no makeup, and her big red curls looked far wilder than I'd seen them so far. I would have thought that Winston looked fine if I hadn't seen him before, but both his button-down shirt and khakis were wrinkled, and his shirt was untucked. From what little I knew of him, I didn't think he even went out looking like that on the weekends.

There was a mirrored column a few feet away

from me—one of the art deco touches in the hotel —but I didn't bother checking how I looked. I knew it was probably rough, but I didn't care. I just wanted this whole mess over with.

No one had answered Eduardo beyond a grunt from Winston, but he took it in stride. "It was a difficult day yesterday. Today will be better."

I hoped he was right. It couldn't possibly be worse.

A PA pulled up in the van and waved us toward her without even coming into the hotel. We filed out and took the same seats we'd sat in for each trip. As soon as the van lurched into motion, Kaitlin clasped her hand to her mouth. I pulled out the box of cereal, tore it open, and passed it to her. She dug straight into it.

We pulled up at the warehouse-turned-TV-studio, climbed out of the van, and followed the PA through the dark maze of hallways to the green room. "Stay here until you're called," she said, sounding bored.

"What are we doing today?" I asked.

"Are we baking?" Suzette asked.

The PA sighed and rolled her eyes. "Stay here until you're called." Then she left, shutting the door behind her.

We waited for a moment in a huddle by the door. Winston, predictably, was the first to go sit down, followed by Eduardo then Kaitlin. I glanced at Suzette, who stared at the door as if she expected it to reopen at any moment. Who knew when we would be summoned? It could be thirty seconds or three hours the way things had gone around here. I went to sit beside Kaitlin.

She was curled up on the couch with her head resting in her hand. I couldn't tell if she was asleep or just comfortable that way.

"You okay?" I asked quietly.

She smiled sadly and nodded.

I squeezed her hand. "You'll make it. You're strong. I haven't known you long, but I know that."

She smiled a little more enthusiastically and squeezed my hand back. "Thanks, Fran."

"You may be a single mom, but you have friends. If not back home, you have them with us."

Tears filled her eyes, but they were happy ones.

I glanced away and noticed Eduardo looking at us. He caught my eye and nodded. He looked tenderly at Kaitlin before looking away. I realized I knew next to nothing about him—or most of the other bakers aside from Kaitlin. And that Suzette had a son who had been born when she was young.

"You said you're from Texas, Eduardo?"

He nodded. "El Paso. My family's lived there for generations. Except me. I came up here. I wanted to see a different part of the country."

"Do you like it?"

"It's very different from El Paso, but yes. The weather, especially, is very different. Fortunately, my kitchen is warm and winter is the busy time of year. I'm the pastry chef at one of the ski resorts."

"Your busy season is opposite mine. I'm on Cape Cod."

Eduardo grinned. It was a very charming grin. "You're right! We'll have to come visit each other sometime. Maybe we can help each other out in our kitchens!"

I began to wonder if this wasn't a better way to get information out of my fellow bakers—not talking about Jeremy Johnson's murder specifically but chatting about our lives. If nothing else, it would be more interesting than staring at the walls until someone decided to come get us or at least tell us what we were doing today. "What about you, Winston?" I turned toward him and smiled.

He grimaced back. "I work here in the city." He named the restaurant, and I was impressed. I'd seen several write-ups about it that glowed about the desserts. I was surprised I didn't recognize his name.

"You live here too?"

He rolled his eyes. "Yes. Back Bay. I can give you the address, too, if you want it."

I smiled, pretending I didn't notice his annoyance. "I'll get it later. I want to put you all on my Christmas card list!"

He looked disgustedly back at his phone. I looked at Suzette, who had finally taken a seat. She fiddled with a pen that had been sitting on the table beside her.

"What about you, Suzette?"

She sighed. "I live near Berklee College of Music, and I work in Cambridge. Teaching, so I can be home for my son. Restaurant hours don't work when you have a child." She looked at Kaitlin. "You're lucky that way. You don't have to worry about losing your job because you can't work and take care of your baby."

I knew better than to ask more. No one else seemed interested in carrying on a conversation, so I let it die.

We had been waiting a while when Winston stood up, stretched, and headed for the door.

"Where are you going?" I asked.

"Why do you care?" He looked at me incredulously and, I thought, a little harshly.

"I just—we're not supposed to leave." I didn't really have a good answer. Part of it was just my natural curiosity, but if I thought about it, it was also partly because I felt it could be important to tell Sergeant Coburn. Did I suspect Winston?

"I'm sure they'll make an exception for a bathroom break. Two cups of coffee this morning." He strode to the door, yanked it open, and disappeared into the hallway.

That broke the dam. We apparently weren't a very rule-following group. Suzette left next then Eduardo, each ostensibly to use the restroom. They eventually wandered back, but the sense that we were locked in the room was gone.

"Is there anything to eat out there?" Kaitlin asked after a while.

"I didn't see anything," Suzette offered.

She sighed and curled herself up more tightly on the couch. I was glad I had grabbed her that box of cereal, but it was small, and that had been a while ago now.

I stood up. "I'll go see if I can find someone to ask." I wanted to help her, yes, but I also saw it as a good opportunity to go poking around for myself. Everyone else had done it, so why shouldn't I?

I headed straight for the big room where craft services had been set up the day before. The tables were still laden, which made me wonder how Suzette hadn't seen all the food. Maybe she just hadn't come this way.

As I got closer, I realized the tables already looked picked over. It was the same food from yesterday—not just the same spread but the same actual food. I was too wary of the fruit to grab any of it for Kaitlin, and I definitely wasn't going anywhere near the chicken salad that was now floating in a bowl of tepid water. I cautiously tried a cracker, but it was hard and stale. I wasn't giving that to Kaitlin.

I went to hunt for more options. There had to be something edible around here somewhere. The craft services food had to have come from some-where, right? And if all else failed, we were on the set of a baking show—I could sneak into the kitchen and grab her some graham crackers or something.

I wandered around, looking for any kind of kitchen or break room or anything that seemed likely to have snacks, but I found nothing and, weirdly, no one. The place was deserted. I heard a voice in the distance and moved farther down the halls in search of its owner. The echoing voice felt creepy—sinister almost—in the maze of hallways, especially compared to the hectic bustle of the previous days.

I was pretty sure I was near the kitchen when I finally found the voice's owner or at least another human being. "Excuse me!" I called. The woman kept walking. Was it my imagination, or was it Veronica Browning? I hurried after her. "Excuse me!"

Another woman popped out of a doorway. I remembered seeing her on set the day before, hovering near Gail and Neil. She looked startled to see me.

"Hi, um, I was looking for a snack or something. Kaitlin needs something to eat and—"

"You're one of the bakers, right?"

"Yes, I'm Fran—"

"What are you doing here?"

"Here on the set or here in the hallway?" I hoped I wouldn't get in too much trouble for being out of the green room, where we'd been told to stay. I reminded myself I wasn't in elementary school anymore. What would "getting in trouble" even look like? Getting kicked off the show? Or worse, winning and being contractually required to go on another one. I should have paid more attention to the contract I'd had to sign.

"Never mind." She waved her hand. "Just go on set and grab something. It's not like we need to worry about the kitchen stock anymore."

"So does that mean we won't be resuming filming?"

She froze, looking at me like a deer caught in the headlights. "Well, um, no... I mean, I don't know yet. A decision hasn't been made, but with Jeremy dead, I mean, a murder... I mean, how can we? Shoot, I shouldn't have said that! Don't—don't tell anyone I said that! It's fine. Everything is fine. Everyone is still getting paid. Everything is fine! There's nothing to worry about. It's fine!" She turned around to go the opposite way down the hallway then apparently realized that wasn't where she should be going and turned again to go back in the room she came from.

"Um, which way is the kitchen?" I called after her.

Her arm poked back into the hallway and pointed in the direction I'd seen the other woman walking. I headed that way and finally recognized the big swinging door to the set. I pushed it open, stepping into the eerily dark room.

The whole very large space—about the size of the softball field in the park near my house—was lit by a single emergency light on the far side of the room. I hesitated, remembering that someone had been murdered yesterday just down the hall and that whoever had done it hadn't been caught. But knowing Jeremy, though only from TV, I suspected that had more to do with him as a person than with someone just looking to kill random people who happened to be in the building.

I took a deep breath and a step forward. "It's fine, Fran. There's nothing to be afraid of," I whispered.

I did not find myself very convincing. Another deep breath. I forced myself to walk toward the wall of ingredients to my right. I had to work even harder to turn my back on the big, dark space so I could find some crackers. I kept picturing someone sneaking up behind me and sinking one of those blue-handled knives into my back. How long would it take for someone to find me? Probably too long for me to survive.

I spun around to survey the empty kitchen.

Anyone could be out there, hiding in the shadows, lurking just where I couldn't see them.

I turned to the shelves again. I wanted to just grab something and run, but the closest thing was a canister of flour, and that wouldn't help Kaitlin's nausea at all. I moved down the shelves, glancing over my shoulder every few seconds. I tried to swallow, but my mouth was dry. I put my hand to my chest. I could feel my heart racing beneath it.

"Just find the crackers, Fran," I whispered.

Finally, I spotted a canister of graham crackers —perfect for crushing up for a pie or cheesecake crust. Also perfect for a snack for a hungry pregnant lady. I grabbed it off the shelf and spun around. I was sure I'd heard something from across the room.

I stared out into the room. Silence. Nothing moved. Nothing made a sound.

The entire kitchen was silhouetted in front of me. Each of our stations was now immaculate, each of our knife blocks sitting on the countertops. The knife blocks that held the knives just like the one that had been used to kill Jeremy. I wondered if the police had thought to check them.

My fear subsided a little at the thought of finding a clue. I stepped forward toward the first station—Eduardo's. The knife block was fully stocked. I checked the drawer that held a few extras and duplicates of the knives we were most likely to use. Everything seemed to be there.

The next one was Kaitlin's. It also looked like everything was there.

I almost skipped my station since I knew I hadn't killed Jeremy, but realized that if the murderer *had* gotten the knife from here, he—or she —didn't necessarily take it from their own station. If he was even one of us. My block and drawer were both fully stocked.

I had to cross the room to get to Winston and Suzette's stations. It made me nervous but not nervous enough to skip it.

I was halfway there when something clattered in the back of the room. My head snapped in the direction of the noise just in time to see a shadow moving in the darkness.

Chapter 20

I FROZE IN TERROR.

I was afraid to move—to even blink—in case somehow, whoever else was in the room didn't already know I was there. And I was afraid to look away for fear that they'd move and I wouldn't see where they went.

It felt like an eternity before I finally felt brave enough to flick my eyes toward the door to see how close it was.

Footsteps.

I looked back into the shadows. Were they different now? I could almost swear they were.

I tried to call out to them, to let them know I knew they were there, but my voice came out as a whisper. I reminded myself that this wasn't my first rodeo—I'd confronted murderers and criminals before. I had plenty of time to run if they tried to come for me. Well, unless they were hiding behind one of the baking stations.

I swallowed hard despite the dryness of my throat, gathered every last shred of courage, and called out again, this time actually managing to make noise. "Hello?"

Nothing.

"I know you're there."

Still nothing. The silence somehow made me think whoever it was out there was both more and less of a threat. More because they were hiding and less because they weren't coming out. Regardless, I was still terrified.

I took a sideways sliding step toward the door, keeping my eyes on the shadows. Another sliding step. Then another. Nothing moved, and no one made a sound.

The door was behind me. All I had to do was turn my back and run. *Turn my back.* I couldn't do it. I started making my sliding steps slowly, steadily backward. Until I caught my hip on the sharp edge of the countertop of one of the baking stations.

I cried out, stumbled forward, bobbled the

canister of graham crackers, and absolutely, definitely heard rapid footsteps moving toward me.

I pulled the canister to my chest and ran. Through the door and down the hall. Around the corner and down the hall toward the green room.

I stopped just before bursting through the door. How would I explain my mad dash and the fact that I was out of breath? I ducked into the single-person bathroom and locked myself in. I leaned against the wall and closed my eyes. I was fine. Everything was fine. It was probably just a PA who was as scared as I was. They probably thought I was the murderer they needed to hide from. Everything was fine.

There was a knock on the door, and I nearly jumped out of my skin. Had I been followed? Was the murderer waiting outside the door to trap me inside and stab me like they'd stabbed Jeremy?

The doorknob rattled, and there was another knock. "Is anyone in there?"

I breathed a sigh of relief at hearing Kaitlin's voice.

"Just a second!" I flushed the toilet and ran the sink in an attempt to recreate a convincing bathroom visit then unlocked the door and opened it for Kaitlin.

She barely looked at me as she darted in, dancing a little on her way. I probably should have skipped the theatrics and just let her come straight in.

I made my way down the hall to the green room. Eduardo looked up at me and smiled. Suzette glanced my way and then resumed examining her fingernails. I sat down on the couch and put the canister of graham crackers beside me. "Where's Winston?"

"Bathroom," Suzette said.

"Again? I was just there and didn't see him."

Suzette's eyebrow went up, whether in curiosity or annoyance, I couldn't tell. She was nearly impossible to read, and I thought she knew it. "There are two bathrooms," she said calmly.

I nodded. I'd actually forgotten that. The other one was farther away, closer to the actual set. Maybe he had gone to that one.

"He has been gone a while," Eduardo said.

Suzette turned her raised eyebrow on him. "Fran was gone a long time too. Are we keeping tabs on everyone now?"

Eduardo shrugged. "I only noticed is all."

I held up the canister of graham crackers.

"These were surprisingly hard to find. I ended up taking them from the set."

Suzette's eyebrow turned to me again.

"A PA said I could."

She looked back at her fingernails.

We'd been holed up together too long. We were starting to get on each other's nerves. Well, we seemed to be getting on Suzette's nerves, anyway, which was making all of us a little touchy.

"I hope Kaitlin's okay," I said when the silence started to get to me. We'd had enough of that the day before.

Suzette raised an eyebrow at me.

"Not keeping tabs. Just concerned. She's been in the bathroom a while. I just hope nothing's wrong."

"Are you always this concerned with everyone else's business? She went to speak to Gail about the filming. I'm sure that's where she is. Happy now?" Suzette continued staring at me until I nodded and looked away to study the carpet.

At first, it looked blue, but when I examined it closely, it had little flecks of pink and green and gray —made of scraps and meant to hide stains, no doubt.

When I dared to look up, I met Eduardo's eyes. He gave me a kind smile. I gave him one back, but I didn't dare try to make conversation. I wasn't up to testing Suzette's patience any further.

I pulled out my phone to see that Matt had texted me.

Sale's pitching and Chris got seats right behind the plate! See you tonight!

And then a separate message.

Hope you're having fun

Fun was exactly the opposite of what I was having. But at least Matt seemed to be. Good for him. I shot him a text back, telling him I was fine and to have fun, even though he didn't seem to need any of my encouragement.

I texted Sammy to check on the café and then Rhonda for a second opinion. Sammy was relentlessly positive and Rhonda brutally honest, so I knew that between the two of them, I'd get a good idea of how things were going.

I checked my email, only to find nothing particularly interesting aside from a couple invoices from vendors, which, to be fair, weren't *interesting* either but did need to be handled. I forwarded them to Sammy with a request for her to pay them and put my phone back into my pocket. Kaitlin and Winston still weren't back.

I glanced around. Suzette was sitting straight up

with her eyes closed, either meditating or taking a very tense, controlled nap. Eduardo was looking at his phone.

I decided to risk provoking Suzette's ire but carefully. I leaned toward Eduardo. He raised his eyes from his phone.

"Kaitlin and Winston have been gone a while, haven't they?" I asked quietly, just in case Suzette actually was asleep.

Her eyes slitted open and flicked in my direction but quickly closed again. She exhaled loudly.

Eduardo had looked up from his phone to meet my eyes. He nodded. "They have been, yes." His voice, too, was low.

"Do you think I should go check on them?"

His eyebrows rose, and he inclined his head.

"It just seems strange, you know? And there was a murder here yesterday."

He glanced at Suzette then the door. "Look for Kaitlin, yes. Winston, I think, is fine."

"Should we both go?"

He hesitated, then he shook his head. "Better that one of us stays here." Anticipating my next question, he added, "She may need a woman's touch."

I was about to protest what at first seemed like

casual sexism, but then I realized he was probably right. Kaitlin was young and pregnant and had found a dead body the day before. I was a decade older than her and had never been pregnant, but I'd dealt with more than my share of dead bodies. Plus, I was nosy and had only offered for Eduardo to come along as a nicety.

I stood up. "I'll be back."

He nodded. Suzette didn't flinch.

In the hall, I glanced around then headed for the bathroom. The door was open, and the room was empty. I walked down the hall toward the set, poking my head through doorways and around corners as I passed, careful not to touch anything just in case the police weren't done checking for fingerprints.

I saw the door with Jeremy Johnson's name on it and shivered. It was eerie to see his dressing room and know that his clothes and belongings were inside but that he'd never be touching them again. For a second, I thought about going inside and looking around, but I didn't know what I'd say if someone saw me. Blame Sergeant Coburn? With my luck, it would be Detective Mulholland that caught me, and he'd probably have me hauled off to the police station before I could even get

Coburn's name out of my mouth. I walked on by even if I wasn't sure that meant I was exercising self-control or giving in to my nerves.

Two doors down was Veronica Browning's dressing room. The light was on and the door cracked open. I hesitated then stepped toward it.

Veronica's voice drifted into the hall. "I understand that, but I have a contract." A pause. "I. Have. A. Contract." Another pause. "No, now you listen. I will not be pushed around. I will not be cowed. I signed on to this show as the head judge, and as the head judge, I say we are continuing. And if you disagree, I'm sure my lawyer will be happy to enlighten you on how *contract law* works. Ugh!"

The door flew open, and Veronica Browning was standing in front of me.

A flutter of emotions flew across her face (the parts that could move, anyway) until she seemed to settle on an approximation of a smile. "Fran, right? Your Boston cream pie was delicious."

I nodded and saw the opportunity. "Thank you. I was wondering—"

Veronica shook her head. "I really can't be caught talking to a contestant. It could give the impression of favoritism."

"Does that mean we'll be finishing the competition?"

She froze, then her eyes narrowed, which looked strange since the corners of them couldn't crinkle. "Of course we're finishing the competition. Why? What have you heard?"

"Well, with Jeremy's death, I just thought—"

She grabbed my arm in a grip startlingly reminiscent of that of my café regular, Mrs. D'Angelo, and pulled me inside her dressing room, shutting the door behind us.

It wasn't a big space, but it was definitely more luxurious than the green room we'd been stuck in. The couch looked plush, and stylish lamps gave off soft light while sitting on actual end tables that didn't look like they'd come from the bargain basement of the cheapest thrift store in town. On the near wall hung a large mirror beside what looked like one of the chairs from hair and makeup, I guessed so that Veronica didn't run the risk of being seen with the bakers. And clothing was strewn across every available surface.

"What have you heard?" she asked again.

"Nothing. I just thought that since Jeremy was murdered—"

Eye rolls were apparently not affected by copious Botox.

"That we wouldn't be able to keep going. Especially since we haven't filmed the judging."

She released me with a wave of her hand. "That's nothing. We can edit him out."

"*Edit him out?*" It seemed callous to edit out a man who had been murdered while filming the very show she now wanted to edit him out of.

"Or do reshoots. None of your desserts were so special that Culinary can't just make replicas for us to judge."

My face must have looked shocked.

"Not that they weren't *delicious*. Yours, anyway. Kaitlin's—" I was surprised to see that Veronica's lip could curl at the memory. "I don't know what Jeremy was thinking, arguing to bring her on. Total impropriety, for one, but also, that cake was"—she waved her hands—"one of the worst things I've ever tasted. And I judged that show where the whole premise is people not being able to bake. Anyway, the cakes just have to *look* like the ones you made for the camera. We'll make it work, whatever." She stopped and looked at me as if she was seeing me for the first time. "Yours was the best, you know."

My heart somehow sank and soared at the same time. I was competitive enough and cared about my reputation enough that of course I wanted to win, but at the same time, I dreaded any possibility of having anything else to do with Baking Network ever again except, of course, watching their programming from the comfort of my couch.

"Classic but not too classic, right?" Veronica continued. "Exactly what we—what *I*—look for. The bourbon was a genius twist. What made you think of it?"

"Well, my boyfriend—"

"Ugh, boyfriends. Liars and cheaters, all of them. Except yours, of course. Probably. I don't know. I've never met him. He's not here, is he?"

I hesitated, not sure if she meant here in Boston or here at the studio.

Before I could decide on her meaning, she rushed on. "Of course he's not. Why would he be? Anyway, I'm sure he's one of the good ones. Maybe *the* good one. There must be *one*." She clapped her hands and looked at me with something approaching sincerity on her face. "It's been great talking to you, Francine, but I have to get back to my show preparations. You can tell your fellow bakers that we *are* continuing and I look forward to tasting all of their bakes."

She smoothly ushered me toward the door, and I let her, not quite sure what to make of everything that had just happened.

The door clicked closed behind me, and I was left standing in the hallway.

I turned to head back the way I had come, slightly mystified.

I stopped outside Jeremy's door. I was sure it had been closed all the way earlier, but now, it was cracked open. The lights were off, but—was that a noise from inside? A kind of shuffle? I took a step closer to the door and listened again. Another soft shuffle.

"Hello?" I called out softly. "Is someone in there?"

Silence.

And then, from inside the room, a short intake of breath.

Someone was in Jeremy Johnson's dressing room.

Chapter 21

"HELLO?" I called again, more assertively this time. A little voice in the back of my head told me I should shut my mouth and leave before I found myself with a Baking Network–branded knife sticking out of my chest, but I had no intention of listening to it.

I stepped toward Jeremy Johnson's dressing room door, reaching out a tentative hand to push it a little farther open.

Another sharp inhale from somewhere inside the room.

It was time to see what I was up against.

I pushed the door all the way open, letting light from the hallway shine in and fall on the figure curled up, sniffling, on the couch.

Kaitlin.

I found the light switch on the wall and flipped it on then stepped inside and latched the door behind me.

"No, leave it off." Kaitlin's voice came out as a whimper.

I flicked the light switch back off. To my surprise, the room didn't fall into complete darkness. A small nightlight plugged into the wall gave off just enough of a glow that I could still see Kaitlin balled up on the couch.

I went over and sat next to her. She curled into me like a child.

"He hated the dark," she whispered. "He always had a nightlight so he could see. I used to tease him about it, but now—now—" Her voice choked on a sob.

"You knew him pretty well, didn't you?" I asked slowly as I started putting the pieces together.

She nodded against my shoulder.

I slid my arm around her. "Was he—" I stopped, afraid to put my thought into words.

"I fell in love with him the first time I saw him on set. I'd seen him on TV, of course, so I knew he was handsome, but I didn't realize how handsome. He took my breath away. I *needed* to be with him."

I rubbed her arm gently, trying to think of what to say. "It feels like that sometimes."

"He felt the same way. He would catch my eye whenever he was on set, and I knew, just *knew*, that he felt it too. Just the way he looked at me. It was like I was naked. Like he was seeing my soul." She took a deep shuddering breath. "The filming was torture. We weren't allowed to even *see* the judges off set, even though we were staying in the same hotel. And he was so good, so honorable, that he didn't want anything to look improper. He said that's why he couldn't vote for me to win. It would have looked bad if anyone found out about—about us afterward. They'd think I only won because I was sleeping with one of the judges."

"*Were* you sleeping with one of the judges?"

She shook her head adamantly. "No. Not then. Not until after." She stopped, and I could see the smile that lit up her face in the dim light. "The night we finished filming, he came to my room. That was when we—" She closed her eyes and took a long, slow breath. I let her feel whatever she needed to feel in the moment. Finally, she opened her eyes again. A faint smile played at her lips. "It was the best night of my life."

"Kaitlin," I started slowly, not sure if I should

say what had come to my mind. I plowed ahead anyway. Blame Coburn or my nosiness. I liked Kaitlin a lot and felt protective toward her, but still. "I might be mixing Jeremy up with someone else, but… wasn't he married?" In fact, I knew I wasn't mixing him up with anyone else. I clearly remembered the day Chloe and Amanda had gleefully huddled over Chloe's phone, looking at some tabloid article about "Professional Grouch Jeremy Johnson's Smoking Hot Wife Caught Eating Another Man's Pastries," which really just meant that some paparazzo had gotten pictures of her eating dessert at a restaurant. Jeremy Johnson had definitely been married. Until yesterday, anyway.

Her face darkened. "I know it wasn't right, but she was awful to him. Always nagging, always complaining about his work schedule. He's a world-famous pastry chef! He judges baking competitions around the world! Of course he's busy! She just doesn't understand him and how important his work is to him." She caught herself and caught a sob in her throat. "*Was.* How important his work *was* to him." She crumpled into me again, covering her face in her hands.

Somehow, a man's mistress didn't seem to be the best one to speak to the state of his marriage. Of course, the word of a man cheating on his wife with a woman half his age didn't seem the most trustworthy source of information about his wife's behavior in their marriage either.

"So she didn't travel with him?"

She shook her head. "No, she stayed in London all the time. She didn't like to travel. And their kids were in school."

I nodded calmly, as if those weren't perfectly good reasons to be annoyed with your husband for traveling all the time. Of course, I wasn't married, but they were at least reasons I could see for her to be complaining about her husband. "Did she know about the two of you?" I asked after a moment.

"He was going to tell her. He was supposed to. He said he would. The—the time just wasn't right. He said he would. But now—now he'll never—we'll never—" She broke down into sobs again.

I pulled her closer and rubbed her arm some more. She slowly regained control of herself again. Talking to her was like riding a roller coaster. Not that I blamed her for her wild mood swings—the poor girl was pregnant and had found her lover murdered the day before, in the middle of a high-pressure baking competition, no less.

Which is what was bothering me. It felt wildly

insensitive, so I waited as long as I could stand it before cautiously asking, "Was Jeremy not concerned about the conflict of interest with you being on *Hometown Showdown*? I mean, since you said he was so worried about it before when you were on *Spring Fling*. It just seems like it would be a bigger conflict now that you're actually... together."

I chose my words carefully, not wanting to assume anything she hadn't already told me, for fear of her shutting down. No matter how much sympathy I had for her plight, there had been a murder, and Sergeant Coburn had asked for my help—okay, not so much my *help*, but he *had* invited me to engage the other bakers in conversation in hopes of them sharing information relevant to the case. And almost anything seemed relevant if it was coming from the victim's mistress.

I felt her shoulders straighten even as she continued leaning against me. "He didn't know I was coming."

"He *didn't know*?" I repeated.

She shook her head. "No, Gail was the one who reached out to me."

"You didn't tell him?" Had she thought it would be a fun surprise?

She hesitated then shook her head. "Like I said,

he's really busy with his filming schedule. And seeing his kids. He loves his kids. It's just his wife who's a pain. I've barely been able to get hold of him lately. I thought about turning the show down —the impropriety and all—but when Gail said he'd be hosting, I realized it was my chance to get to spend a few days with him. So of course I said yes!"

"Did he know you were here before they came on set?"

"Of course!" she said, as if anything about this was obvious at this point. "I knew one of the Pas from *Spring Fling*, and I convinced her to tell me where his room was. I went to surprise him the night we got here."

I waited, but she didn't offer anything else. "How did he react?" I asked finally.

She grimaced. "He wasn't super happy about it. 'Cause of how it would look, you know? But he said I couldn't drop out, because then Gail would find out about us, and then Baking Network would find out, and his career would be in trouble. Because people would think he couldn't be impartial, you know?"

I nodded, thinking back to every episode of every Jeremy Johnson show I'd ever seen and questioning whether he'd been having affairs with anyone on those shows too. I'd loved to hate him for years, but now I was starting to just hate him. I clearly wasn't alone in that sentiment, since he was dead.

"He told me I wouldn't win, 'cause that would be wrong and all, but I kind of knew that before I got here anyway. And I was okay with that." She shrugged. "I just wanted to see him and be with him."

"And... were you?" I asked carefully.

She nodded. "I stayed in his room with him."

Suddenly, I had an idea. "Kaitlin, did you ever hear him on the phone with anyone? Or did he maybe mention someone who had a grudge against him?"

She shook her head. "No, no one. He talked to his wife and kids, but that was it. He did seem really distracted and kind of distant, and he wasn't super lovey like usual, but, I mean, he was under a lot of stress with the show and stuff, so I didn't think too much of it. Like I said, I was just glad to finally be with him again. I hadn't seen him for months!"

I took a deep breath. Kaitlin was young and in love, and that had a tendency to make people stupid. "Did you tell the police any of this?"

"No, I—I was scared. Jeremy had a reputation.

If I told the police, it could get out, and people would think poorly of him."

As far as I was concerned, he deserved to have people think poorly of him. But that was neither here nor there. There was one last thing I had to ask. "Kaitlin, did you kill Jeremy?"

She gasped. "Of course not! I could never hurt my baby's father!"

Chapter 22

KAITLIN and I walked slowly back to the green room, where we were supposed to have been all along. I tried to ignore the fact that she was newly wearing a sweater that smelled of men's expensive cologne and was distinctly oversize on her petite frame. I had my arm around her shoulder, supporting her half emotionally and half physically, and could feel that the sweater was made of cashmere, expensive cashmere at that.

"You don't think I'm a bad person, do you, Fran?"

I took a deep breath. I wanted to be honest with her but didn't want to upset her. "I think you're a talented and attractive young woman who has a big future in front of her, but you have to be careful that you don't let people take advantage of you."

She was quiet for a moment then asked, "You think he was taking advantage of me?"

"I don't know. But I think he told you some things you wanted to hear in hopes that he would get what he wanted."

We were almost at the green room door when she said in nearly a whisper, "He didn't want the baby."

My chest tightened with sadness. I stopped and turned her to face me. "He told you that?"

"He said he wasn't going to ruin his life over some illegitimate brat." She sniffled. "That was really why I came. I told him about the baby as soon as I found out, and he hung up on me. I thought that if he saw me and saw that it was really real, saw how my body was changing, he'd change his mind. He'd want to be with me and take care of his baby—*our* baby."

"But he didn't."

Her lip quivered. "He said he never wanted to see me again." Her tears spilled over, and she crumpled into my arms. "I just wanted us to be a family."

I held her while she cried. Suzette came out and

looked at us with actual concern. I rubbed Kaitlin's back and nodded to tell Suzette that we were okay. Suzette hovered in the hallway. I raised my eyebrows in silent question. She made a face as if she was fighting back tears. I inclined my head toward us. Kaitlin needed the support of women.

Suzette came over and put her hand on Kaitlin's back. Kaitlin looked up at her. Suzette looked at her with genuine sorrow in her eyes. "I've been there. I know."

Kaitlin put her head back on my shoulder, and the three of us stood there in an almost group hug for a long time.

Kaitlin's tears finally faded to soft whimpers then sniffles. She picked up her head, wiped her eyes, and squared her shoulders. She took a deep breath and looked from me to Suzette and back. "I'll be okay. *We*'ll be okay."

I smiled encouragingly and nodded. She had a lot of growing up to do, but I was hopeful for her. And I hoped that I could be there for her and her baby.

"You will be," Suzette said. "You're strong, and your baby will be strong. His father may be gone, but you make your own family. And you can start with us."

I wondered if Suzette knew about Jeremy like she'd known about Kaitlin's pregnancy. Had Kaitlin told her? I didn't think so. Everything Kaitlin had said to me had seemed very much as if she was getting it off her chest, a dam breaking, a letting out of things she'd been keeping pent up. It wouldn't have come out like that if she'd said it before.

"I love kids." Eduardo's voice came from the door behind us. I turned to see him and Winston and wondered how long they'd been standing there. "I don't get to be Tio Eduardo enough with all my nieces and nephews back in El Paso. I'd love to have you and your little one out to the resort. We'll make a little snow bunny of her." His eyes had a look in them that made me wonder if he didn't want to be a little more than *tio* to Kaitlin's baby.

"You've got friends all over the state now," Winston offered. It wasn't quite the joyous invitation Eduardo had given, but it was a lot coming from him.

"You and your baby are going to be just fine," I said with a smile.

A dramatic throat-clearing sound came from behind us. We all jumped and turned to see Detective Mulholland glaring at us with his arms crossed.

Sergeant Coburn stood behind him with his hands in his pockets.

"Fran?" Coburn jerked his head down the hallway.

I patted Kaitlin's shoulder and went to follow Coburn.

"Is there a reason you're all standing around in the hallway?" Mulholland asked the rest of them as we walked away.

Coburn led me to a door with "Gail Malinsky, Executive Producer" on it. He pushed the door opened and motioned for me to step inside.

Gail's office was tiny, her desk small and messy. It was a wonder she managed to fit two chairs inside it. I took the one wedged into the corner, leaving the one behind the desk for Coburn, although watching him squish himself into it made me wonder if his larger frame wouldn't have been more comfortable on my side.

"How're you holding up?" he asked, trying to arrange his elbows on the too-close table. He gave up and tried to sit back but didn't have room for that either. He ended up sitting ramrod straight with his hands as close as he could get to folded in front of him, which was basically also pressed up against his chest. He looked mildly ridiculous but somehow completely unbothered.

"I'm okay." I tried to keep my face under control as my mind raced to decide whether—and what—to tell him about Kaitlin.

"Yeah?" He nodded. "Mike said you were pretty tough."

"How are *you* holding up?"

He chuckled quietly. "I'm a homicide detective. I'll be good when I close this case and get to go home, sit in my favorite chair with a glass of good bourbon, and watch a ball game without thinking about how somebody died."

"You'd get along with my boyfriend. His two favorite things are bourbon and ball games."

"Oh yeah? Has he ever tried Revere's Harbor? They age the bourbon in barrels out at sea. They send the boats in and out of Boston Harbor. Their labels have a church steeple with two lights in it. 'Two if by sea,' right? Kind of gimmicky, but it's really smooth. One of my favorites."

"I'm not sure if he's tried it. I'll have to ask. It sounds right up his alley, though."

He studied me for a moment. "You find out anything I should know? About the case?"

I took a deep breath. My time to decide what

I'd share was up. "Kaitlin had an affair with Jeremy Johnson. She's pregnant with his baby." A raising of his eyebrows was Coburn's only reaction. I blathered on. "He didn't want the baby. Or anything to do with her anymore. He didn't know she was coming here. But I don't think that's a motive for her to kill him."

A faint smile played at the corner of his mouth. "If anything, I'd say it's the opposite. Anything else?"

I thought for a moment. I could tell him a fair amount about my fellow bakers' personal lives, where they lived, and where they were from, but none of that was anything he wouldn't have been able to find out on his own and probably already knew from his interviews. I shook my head. "No. I'm sorry."

"Nothing to be sorry for. You did exactly what I asked." He slapped his hands down on the table and moved to get up, but the spot he was in was so tight he had to lean over the desk and extract one leg at a time.

I opened the door and tried to let him go out first, but there was no way he could fit past me. We finally made it out of Gail's office, and he walked me back down the hall toward the green room.

"Do you happen to know if we're going to keep filming?" I asked. Short of asking Gail herself, whom I hadn't seen since before the murder, Coburn seemed like the next-best person. He'd at least know if we were *allowed* to keep shooting.

He glanced behind us before answering. "I know more about this than I've ever wanted to, but word is the network has no intention of continuing, but there are some contract issues they need to sort out before it's official. You didn't hear that from me, though. Apparently, it could cause some issues if word gets out too soon."

I remembered Veronica's screaming fit on the phone earlier and had a feeling I knew whom the contract issues involved.

The green room was empty when we got to it. Coburn led me past it. "They're sending you all back to the hotel for the day. Must have already loaded them up."

Sure enough, outside, my fellow bakers were already in the idling van.

Coburn patted me on the back as I walked past him and out the door. "Thanks, Fran."

I smiled and waved goodbye then climbed into my spot in the van. Eduardo smiled, and Suzette gave me a slight nod. The driver quietly muttered "finally" as Winston shot me a glare. I ignored them and buckled up next to Kaitlin. She was already asleep.

I pulled out my phone just to see what I'd missed. My heart lifted to see a message from Matt and then fell when I read it.

Hey babe! Realized when we got here it's a doubleheader! Won't be back at the hotel until late. Hope everything's good. Love you.

I bit my tongue and batted away tears. Hadn't Matt come on this trip to be with *me*? To spend time with *me*? He'd spent more time with Chris than he had with me, *especially* when I only counted waking hours. What was he even thinking? Even if we had actually been filming today, I would have been back at the hotel long before him. I might not have liked baseball, but I knew how late the games ended. And that was assuming Matt and his friend didn't decide to hit a bar afterward. Who knew what time he'd really be back? There was no way I was going to sit in the hotel and feel sorry for myself all night.

"What do you guys want to do for dinner tonight? I think we should go somewhere interesting."

The other bakers looked around at each other.

Winston looked at the PA driving the van. "We good to do whatever we want?"

"Do what you want as long as you're around when someone sends me to get you in the morning," the driver muttered.

Eduardo tapped on his phone. "There's a Mexican-Asian fusion restaurant a friend of mine owns near the hotel. He can get us in at eight."

Except for Kaitlin, who was still asleep, we all agreed.

"Fran, is your boyfriend still here? Do we need a seat for him?"

I pushed down my emotions and clenched my teeth. "No."

Chapter 23

DINNER WAS DELICIOUS, and I mostly managed to ignore how upset I was about Matt ditching me yet again. Eduardo seemed to sense my dark mood and took it as his mission to keep the tone light for my sake and Kaitlin's, although he did seem to take a special interest in cheering up Kaitlin. For the entire two hours we were at the restaurant, eating his friend's surprisingly delicious Japanese-inspired Mexican food, he regaled us with entertaining stories about growing up in El Paso and the antics he and his seemingly endless number of sisters and cousins had gotten up to. Kaitlin and I dissolved into fits of laughter at least twice when he launched into impressions of his *abuelita*, who, to hear him tell it, was the wisest and most dryly sarcastic person to ever walk the face of the earth.

Suzette and Winston, seated at the opposite end of the table from Eduardo, were unsurprisingly aloof, though Suzette at least seemed to be half listening to Eduardo's stories and chuckled out loud a time or two. Winston mostly stared into space and looked as if he was just waiting for the meal to be over. I didn't understand how someone who was a pastry chef could seem so uninterested in food, especially as unusual a combination as Asian and Mexican. Pastry was obviously a whole different animal from savory, but part of making desserts in a restaurant was complementing the head chef's work, so a pastry chef usually had some level of background or interest in regular cooking. I'd never met one who didn't, as a matter of fact.

Finally, after four courses and several bonus sharing dishes, "compliments of the chef," we left the restaurant and made our way back to the hotel. We collectively decided to walk, as it was a pleasant evening and getting a rideshare for five people was more trouble than we wanted to deal with—well, more trouble than anyone besides Winston wanted to deal with, but he eventually gave in to the majority's opinion. Besides, Boston traffic was always bad enough that it almost seemed safer to jaywalk across the highway during rush hour than navigate the city in a car, especially the car of someone you'd never met.

Despite Winston and Suzette being the locals, Kaitlin, Eduardo, and I led the way in a loose huddle, Eduardo still telling stories, while the two of them lingered behind. A couple of times, I thought I heard one of their voices raised, but when I turned around, they both seemed calm, if annoyed. That was more or less par for the course with them, though.

When we got back to the hotel, Winston and Suzette went straight up to their rooms, but Eduardo, Kaitlin, and I decided we wanted to stop at the bar for a drink. Eduardo ordered a Boston sour, which was apparently a version of a whiskey sour made with an egg white, I got an old fashioned, and Kaitlin ordered a Shirley Temple. The bartender did his best to disguise his surprise after Eduardo's and my order, but Kaitlin just smiled and patted her belly. The bartender smiled back, winked, and conveniently forgot to charge her for it.

The three of us chatted for a while and mostly ignored the basketball game that was on the TVs above the bar. I did catch Eduardo looking at it a few times, but he seemed more interested in making us laugh than anything else. We had a brief debate about ordering a second round—a recipe for disaster if the PAs came calling early in the morning—but Kaitlin had yawned enough times that we decided it was best for all our sakes to call it a night.

We were crossing the lobby to the elevator bank when I heard a familiar voice call out.

"Hey, gorgeous!"

I turned around to see Matt with another man, who I assumed was his friend Chris.

Despite my hurt feelings earlier, I broke into a smile and, slightly embarrassingly, ran across the lobby and into his arms.

"You okay, babe?" he asked after kissing me and brushing my hair back out of my eyes.

"Yeah. Just a long day." I rested my head on his chest. I had so much to tell him, so many feelings to sort through and questions to get his opinion on. Sometimes, just saying things out loud to him made everything seem simple and logical. It must have been his engineer brain.

"Us too!" he said, as if sitting at a baseball game was anything like what I'd been through. "The second game went into extra innings!"

There was that unhappy feeling again.

Pushing it aside, I reintroduced Matt to Kaitlin and Eduardo. Likewise, he introduced us all to Chris. "We were going to sit in the bar and watch the Celtics game, if you guys want to hang out," Matt suggested.

I bit my tongue—literally—to keep from saying something embarrassing in front of everyone.

"They're playing the Suns, right? That's my team! I'd love to join if you don't mind!" Eduardo said with his characteristic enthusiasm.

Kaitlin's eyes visibly glazed over. "I'm going to go to bed."

They all looked at me while I debated internally. Join the boys' night or go to bed alone? I decided they'd had enough boys' time. "I'll hang out for a little while."

Matt's grin warmed me inside. I hadn't even realized I'd been afraid of his disappointment until I didn't see it.

Kaitlin bade us goodnight and headed for the elevators. Matt slung his arm across my shoulders as the rest of us went over to the bar. Eduardo and I took the same seats we'd been in previously, with Matt beside me and Chris on Matt's other side. Eduardo ordered another Boston sour, but I decided to play it safe and asked for a glass of red wine. Matt and Chris both ordered bourbon. I was about to ask if they'd ever tried the Revere's Harbor that Sergeant Coburn had told me about, but as soon as I opened my mouth, something happened in the basketball game that caused Matt, Chris, and most of the hotel bar to cheer. Eduardo good-naturedly hung his head and took their ribbing. I closed my mouth and decided to save the question for later.

It didn't take too many instances of Eduardo leaning back to talk to Chris while I leaned forward or me leaning back while Matt leaned forward to talk to Eduardo for them to get tired of the seating arrangement. Eduardo moved down to Chris's other side so they could talk basketball unimpeded, although to me, it mostly sounded like heckling since they were rooting for opposing teams. Not that I could hear it too well anyway since Matt had his back almost completely turned to me.

After a while, I got tired of feeling like the third wheel in our group of four and told Matt I was heading upstairs. He almost managed to look disappointed but not so much that he offered to come up with me. Eduardo had excused himself to the bathroom, and I was tired of waiting for him to come back, so I asked Matt to tell him goodnight for me. I told Chris it was nice to meet him, gave Matt a kiss, and headed for the elevators.

It seemed to take forever for one to arrive, even though there were four of them. The lights above each one changed, but none came to the lobby level. It didn't help my frustration any. When one set of doors finally opened, I punched my floor number and leaned back against the wall. Blame the long day or the two glasses of wine (one at dinner) and one cocktail, but I was getting more exhausted by the second.

I barely remembered to check the floor number when the doors opened. I'd made that mistake already once on the trip—all the floors looked the same. I walked down the hallway toward my room. It was the last one on the left before the hallway turned to make one of the arms of the building's U-shape. For a second, I thought I saw movement at the end of the hall but realized it was probably just my half-drunk, completely exhausted imagination or, more likely, someone who had gotten off an elevator rounding the corner to go to their room.

I patted the rear pocket of my jeans to make sure my key card was there and pulled it out. I held it to the door. The little light didn't turn green. I pulled it away and tried again. And again. I absolutely did not feel like walking all the way back downstairs to get Matt's key or deal with fixing mine. *Was* I on the right floor? I checked the room number to confirm it was correct and tried again. Bingo! This time, the light turned green and the door unlocked. I popped the door open, pushed the key into my back pocket, and took a step inside just as something slammed hard into my back.

Chapter 24

MY FOREHEAD HIT THE DOOR, sending a flash of pain through my skull. The door handle caught my hip as whatever—whoever—was behind me pushed me into the room.

The hit had thrown me off-balance, and I tumbled to the floor. Not a single light was on in the room, and the light-blocking curtains were closed. The only light came in from the hallway.

I got to my knees, but a foot to my backside knocked me back down. My shoulder slammed into the bathroom doorframe.

The pain froze my left arm, but I thought that if I could just get into the bathroom, I could close myself in.

I used my right arm to push myself up and start

to turn, but the foot kicked me down again. For a split second, I saw my attacker silhouetted against the hallway light, but then the door slammed shut, and I could see nothing at all.

I hoped that they couldn't either.

I tried to get up but got knocked down again, this time scraping my arm down the corner of the dresser. My shirt tore with the pressure.

I half crawled, half inched my way farther into the room, trying desperately to get away. I thought I had to be getting close to the other side of the room when the attacker grabbed my hair, pulled me back, and then shoved me down to the floor. I tried to catch my breath, but a boot or heavy shoe pressed into my back, squishing the air out of me. It lifted and came back down hard, knocking the wind out of me altogether.

The attacker grabbed my left shoulder—the one that had slammed into the doorframe—and flipped me over onto my back. Now the foot pressed into my diaphragm.

I realized I was going to die.

And I refused to die.

I swung my hands, trying to grab on to any part of my attacker that I could. I tried to scratch at their legs but couldn't do much through their heavy jeans. I was now pretty sure whoever was attacking me was a man.

His foot lifted and came back down on my abdomen.

I clenched my hands into fists and swung at his legs. If I couldn't scratch, maybe I could hit. One blow caught him just hard enough right where it hurt that he stumbled back a little. I kicked my legs up and got him more solidly. Not enough to bring him to the ground but enough to give me a second to scramble backward.

My eyes were starting to get used to the faint light coming in from under the door and through the crack in the curtains.

I could just see the outline of him as he came at me again and managed to roll away just in time. He slammed into the sliding glass door that led to a balcony I hadn't even had a second to enjoy.

I got to my feet and tried to run for the door but tripped on the bed. He grabbed my hair again, yanking me off my feet then throwing me against the dresser. I bounced off it and onto the floor, bringing the TV down on top of me.

He shoved it aside and kicked me again, getting my leg this time. The TV wasn't heavy, but it was now wedged under the bed and on top of my arm, pinning me in place for him to kick me again. I tried to roll under it to use it as a shield. He kicked me in the base of my spine.

I let myself fall onto my back and kicked at him again. I missed, and he stomped on my shin.

I pushed myself back with the leg that hurt less. He kicked again, hitting my hip. And again, hitting my side.

A whimper squeezed out of my lips, and I realized the only chance I stood was if someone came to help me. I tried to scream, but the only sound that came out was little more than a whimper. I tried again and managed a squeak.

He grabbed the TV and pulled it out from under the bed. I thought for a second that he was going to throw it down on me as he lifted it high above his head, but he threw it toward the bed instead.

I tried to scoot back some more, taking advantage of him momentarily being focused on destroying something else. I tried again to scream but only managed a whispered, "Help."

"No one's coming to help you."

I recognized the voice. I didn't know why he was here, why he wanted to kill me. Oh God, was it because he'd seen me talking to Coburn? I never dreamed—he must have killed Jeremy, too, but why?

He grabbed me by the hair again, this time lifting me to my feet. He pulled my hair back so I was looking straight up and hovered his face inches above mine. "I won't let you hurt her." He was so close I could feel his breath in my mouth.

He jerked my head back again then let go of my hair.

For a split second, I thought he was letting me go, that this was all just a warning.

Then his hands went to my throat, and he started to squeeze.

First, I tried to scream, but I couldn't get the air out or in.

Then I tried to scratch at his hands, but his grip only tightened.

I tried to kick him, but he didn't even flinch.

I scratched at his face, but he moved his head out of my reach.

If I was going to die, the least I could do was make sure his DNA was under my fingernails.

I scratched every part of his flesh I could until my arms got so heavy that I felt as if I was swimming in bread dough.

The room seemed to get brighter with flashing lights everywhere.

There was a ringing that was louder than anything but my pulse in my ears.

He was putting me down, or was he lifting me up? My body was so heavy, and his hands were the only thing keeping me from collapsing.

What would Matt think? What would Matt think when he found me? I hoped he didn't find me. I hoped he didn't—

"What the hell?"

The pressure on my neck lightened. The flashing lights dimmed. The ringing faded.

I could see Winston's face clearly in the light from the hallway for just one deafening heartbeat before he flung me down on the bed.

A grunt from the doorway as Winston shoved past Matt.

Then a scuffle, a slap, and a thud.

Then Matt's voice and his face hovering over me. "Franny!"

I looked into his beautiful brown eyes and let mine close.

Chapter 25

FOR A WHILE AFTER THAT, my memories were hazy.

Matt shouting. Chris asking if I was conscious. Feet running down the hall. A woman yelling.

I remember the ceiling lights going by and the elevator. A man leaning over me, promising I was going to be okay.

Matt saying they got him.

More people shouting. A monitor beeping. My body getting cold and then warm again. A sharp pain. Something covering my face. I couldn't breathe, and then I could. Air! Air! So much air! It was rushing into my lungs without me even trying.

A metallic noise. My body shaking. More lights

flashing overhead. Heavy footsteps. Quiet voices. Matt's hand on mine.

And then—sleep.

When I woke up, everything hurt. Every single inch of my body. I barely wanted to move my eyes, but I managed to lift a finger.

That must have been enough.

Matt jumped up and shouted, "She's awake!"

A nurse came in and started fussing around me. "How're you doing, honey?"

I looked up at her and opened my mouth. Just that motion sent searing pain down my throat.

"No, no, don't try to talk, honey. I'll give you some medicine and let you sleep some more, okay?" I could hear her moving beside me, then she patted my hand. "Let's let her rest a little bit longer, okay?"

I heard Matt's voice say, "Okay," then felt the scruff of his unshaven face as he kissed my hand.

And I slept again.

The next time, no one made me go right back to sleep. Whether that was because I was medically ready or because Sergeant Coburn had decided that was the way it was going to be, I didn't know. Whatever the reason, when I awoke, instead of Matt clutching my hand with devotion, I saw

Coburn staring out the window of my hospital room.

"Can I help you?" I whispered. I hadn't meant to whisper, but that was all I could get out.

He turned around with an expression of pleasant surprise. "Don't try to talk," he said, holding his hands out.

He was the second person to tell me that.

"You're going to be pretty hoarse for a while from the—" He gestured at his throat as if hearing the word "strangulation" would be worse than experiencing it. "I'll need to get your statement, but it can wait a few days until you're up to it. What you need to know now is that we got him. Well, your friend Chris got him. Knocked him out with one punch as he tried to flee. Anyway, he confessed to everything. The assault on you, obviously, but also the Johnson murder. Said he didn't like how the judging went, so he killed him. Doesn't make sense to me, but what do I know?" He shrugged. "I've seen murders that made even less sense. I just investigate; I don't have to understand 'em." He sighed heavily. "Uh, look, Fran. I feel like I bear some responsibility for this. If I hadn't asked you to—"

I tried to argue with him, to say that I probably

would have gotten myself involved anyway, but the feeling of knives slicing my throat stopped me.

"I should have seen this coming, and I didn't. To be honest with you, we were looking at one of the PAs. Apparently, he and Johnson had a long-running feud, and threats had been exchanged both ways. That seemed like where the evidence was pointing. But I was wrong, and I'm sorry."

I appreciated his words, but my still-foggy brain felt as if something was off. But everything felt off. My throat, my ribs, my head.

Coburn's phone rang. He pulled it out of his jacket pocket and looked at it. "I have to take this. But I'll be back." He walked to the door but stopped just before going through it. "Mike Stanton would have killed me if I let anything happen to you." With that, he put his phone to his head and stepped into the hall. "Coburn."

I closed my eyes. It didn't make sense. But what didn't make sense? Nothing made sense. I had a vague feeling that I'd had so much pain medicine that the alphabet wouldn't make sense.

My door creaked. I opened my eyes.

A frizzy mop of red hair came into the room, leaving the door open. I hadn't known it was possible for Suzette to look so disheveled. She had dark circles under her eyes that were pronounced enough that they could only have come from a combination of stress, lack of sleep, and days-old mascara. The T-shirt she had on was dirty, too big, and twisted, as if she'd put it on backward and in the dark.

She sat down in the chair next to me and took my hand.

"I'm so glad you're okay." Her voice was hoarse, and at this distance, I could see how red her eyes were. She really hadn't slept. "I didn't know. I had no idea. I tried—I tried to stop him, but he gets these ideas in his head, and nothing you say or do can get through to him. He—he just —you have to understand. He loves Jackson. Loves him like his own. And he never—he couldn't—I didn't mean to do it, you know. It—it just happened. Kaitlin and the baby—I mean, don't get me wrong, I knew coming here—I just wanted—I never dreamed he would try to hurt you." She looked down at her hands, still clasping mine.

I was hallucinating. I had to be hallucinating, right? They must have given me something for pain that was making me hallucinate. Nothing this messy Suzette clone was saying made any sense. Even less sense than whatever Coburn had said about Winston and the judging.

I tried to shake my head, but my neck could barely move. "What?" I managed to whisper.

She looked up, and I saw the tears streaming down from her brown eyes. "Winston was just trying to protect me. He was absolutely sure you knew, even though I told him you didn't. He kept going on about it. I told him he was wrong. But he wouldn't listen. He just wanted to protect me! He kept saying that you knew. That you were going to turn me in. He said that Jackson couldn't lose his mom when he already didn't have a dad. And he was right. But I had to do it. I couldn't let her go through what I'd gone through. He'd already done enough harm. But I couldn't put her through watching him on TV and reading articles about him and his wife and his happy family. It destroys you, seeing him act like a devoted family man while he can't even be bothered to acknowledge his own son."

"You knew?" I whispered.

"Of course I knew! I knew the minute I saw her! She was just like me the day I walked into his bakery for the first time. Young, blond, and stupid. He likes them blond, you know. And young.

Because that means they're still too stupid to see through him. I couldn't let her go through that." She sniffed and wiped her nose then grabbed back on to my hand. "At first, I was just going to warn her. Try to keep her away. But then I realized he'd already gotten a hold of her. That he'd already— that she was pregnant. And I knew I had to stop him. I don't regret it. You know, he had the audacity to pretend he didn't remember me? I had to actually tell him. 'I'm Susan Connors! Remember me? Remember our *baby*?' You know what he said? 'My lawyer pays for that.' *That*. He called our son a *that*. So I stabbed him. Because I deserved better. And Jackson deserved better. And Kaitlin and her baby deserve better than a man who calls his child a *that*."

A motion behind her caught my eye, and I looked up, behind her.

She froze. And deflated. Her eyes closed. She let go of my hand. Her head fell to her chest.

"Suzette Collins, AKA Susan Connors." Coburn stepped from behind the curtain by the door, pulling his handcuffs out of his belt. "Please stand up and put your hands behind your back."

Tears poured out of her closed eyes as she stood up.

"You're under arrest for the murder of Jeremy Johnson. You have the right to remain silent. Anything you do say…" Coburn put the handcuffs around Suzette's wrists. He nodded sadly at me and continued reading her her rights as he led her out of the room.

Chapter 26

"WAIT, so Winston attacked you, but Suzette killed Jeremy?"

My first day back at the café, we'd closed early so that I could fill everyone in at once on everything that had happened at *Hometown Showdown*.

Sammy and Rhonda knew most of it from conversations we'd had when they came to visit me while I convalesced at home, but I knew I had to fill the girls in, too, if I didn't want the rumor mill to run wild. The news reports had been surprisingly vague, and because I'd been a victim, my name had been left out altogether. But Cape Bay was a small town, and everyone knew that I'd been hospitalized and then resting at home. Rhonda had already heard from one of her boys that there was a rumor

I'd gotten into a knife battle, so it was best to get the truth out there before speculation got even more out of control.

That was also why we were discussing it on the oceanfront patio of my favorite Mexican restaurant —so that if anyone overheard, at least they'd be overhearing my version instead of a second- or third-hand one.

I nodded at Becky. "Yes. Winston attacked me because he thought I knew Suzette killed Jeremy."

"Because they're together." She held the first two fingers of each hand against each other in a literal representation of the word "together."

I nodded again. "Apparently, they'd been living together for ten years. Jackson—that's Suzette's son —thought of Winston like his father."

"And now the poor boy has no one." Rhonda's face was pained.

The first thing she'd asked when I told her the story was who was going to take care of Jackson now that his father was dead, his mother was in jail for his father's murder, and his de facto stepfather was in jail for attempted murder. Of me. The answer was that he was now with his maternal grandparents, which Rhonda had been relieved to hear. She'd been afraid he'd ended up in foster care or—possibly worse—being shipped across the Atlantic to live with his dead father's wife and half-siblings he'd never met.

"What about the show?" Daria asked. "You didn't finish filming, did you?"

It felt like quite a jump in tone, but they were Baking Network–obsessed teenagers. I was almost jealous that, at their age, reality television was more interesting than cheating spouses and murder.

"No," I said a little too emphatically.

The girls laughed. "I'm sure you were *so* disappointed," Chloe teased.

I shrugged and smiled. "The competitive side of me is a little disappointed, but the side of me that has no interest in ever being on TV is very, very happy."

"I would have told them they need to put me on another show," Becky said.

"Hundred percent!" Amanda agreed.

"Nooo. Not for me. I'm not even sure I want to enter a local baking competition."

Sammy gave me a knowing look. "I'll just have to enter the café on your behalf, then." She knew I was a sucker for anything that would improve the café's business.

"Anyway! Common sense prevailed, and *Home-*

town Showdown is not happening anytime soon. And definitely not our episode."

The girls jeered good-naturedly.

"But! They divided the prize money between the three of us who did *not* try to kill anyone."

"On the condition that you sign an NDA," Rhonda muttered.

"It only covers press interviews," I murmured back. "I double-checked."

"How are you going to spend it?" Chloe asked.

"I'm not sure yet." I'd actually already put a chunk of it into a present for Matt, but I didn't think that would be exciting to them.

"I'd go on vacation," Daria said.

"Ooh, to the Bahamas!" Becky suggested.

"Or Hawaii!" Amanda said excitedly.

They batted around their ideas for how to use the money. After beach vacations, they suggested Europe then Japan then moved on to things like a car or a house—neither of which the actual prize money would come even close to paying for, but I didn't want to burst their bubbles. When I gave myself time to think about it, I thought I'd probably use it to buy some new furniture for my house or maybe invest it in the café. I'd wanted to spruce things up and expand our offerings for a while, and while it wasn't a ton of money, the infusion of cash from Baking Network would help. That wouldn't interest them, either, based on their new ideas of "designer wardrobe" and "shopping spree."

They'd circled back around to vacation ideas ("Vacation home in the mountains!") when I glanced at the time on my phone. "Welp, it's been fun catching you guys up, but I have to get going! I'm supposed to meet Matt in ten minutes." I started to stand up but stopped partway to catch my breath. Of all my injuries—mostly cuts and bruises —the broken ribs were proving the hardest to recover from. Except for the bruised throat, of course. That still hurt to the touch and if I tried to talk too much or too loudly.

Sammy and Rhonda stood up on either side of me and took my arms. "We'll walk you out," Rhonda said.

"The gift bag—" I gestured under my chair.

Sammy reached down and grabbed it for me. "I'll carry it." She carried it in one hand and put her other arm around me.

They slowly walked me to the door. I didn't really need that much help, but I did appreciate it.

We stopped at the hostess stand so I could pay for our meal, and then they walked me out of the restaurant and around the side to the edge of the boardwalk.

"So, are you feeling better about things between you and Matt now that you know he was secretly auditioning you for Baking Network?" Sammy asked.

I shrugged then winced. Anything that jostled my ribs or my bruised collarbone was painful. They waited for me to catch my breath. "Kind of. He's still acting weird. But I guess, maybe—" I was going to shrug again but stopped myself just in time. By the time I learned not to do it, I'd probably be healed.

"Maybe what?" Rhonda asked.

"I don't know. Maybe it's stress or something."

"I'd guess it's pretty stressful to walk in on someone trying to murder your girlfriend."

"Yeah, but—" I bit my lip.

"But?"

I looked at them with welling-up eyes. "Just the way he's been acting. I'm not sure he actually *wants* to be my boyfriend anymore. I know it was him trying to get me on the show at first, but the whole time in Boston, it was like he was avoiding me. He was out with his friend or his friend and his wife all the time. One night, he actually told me their dinner reservation was only for three people so I couldn't come. And then he's just been antsy since we've been home. Something's going on, and unless he's trying to put me on TV again, the only thing I can think is that he wants to break up."

Sammy and Rhonda exchanged a look.

"You guys know something, don't you?"

"We know that Matt loves you," Rhonda said a little too quickly.

I looked at Sammy. She nodded a little too quickly too. These two were supposed to be my best friends, but they were definitely hiding something.

"Now, wipe your tears and go meet him." Rhonda produced a tissue out of her bottomless mom-purse.

I wiped my eyes. "Are there more for when he breaks my heart ten minutes from now?"

She pulled out a whole pack of tissues. I shoved them into my pocket. Sammy handed me the gift bag.

"Thank you, guys. I love you."

"We love you too."

They each gave me a gentle hug and watched as I walked down the boardwalk and onto the beach.

I was a little wobbly walking across the sand at

first, which did nothing for my sore ribs, but I managed.

Matt wasn't far down the beach—a concession to my injury—but he was facing the water and didn't see me approaching until I was almost next to him. When he did, he jumped up. I'd never seen him looking so nervous in my life.

"Here, have a seat!" He motioned at the blanket he'd been sitting on.

"Well, first, this is for you." I held out the bag. If he was going to break up with me, at least I'd be going out gracefully.

His eyebrows pulled together in confusion, but he took the bag from me and pulled out the contents. His eyes got wide. "Revere's Harbor? Ten years old? That's their first bottling! That must have cost you a fortune!"

I started to shrug but caught myself. "I wanted to do something nice for you."

"You're amazing, Franny, you know that?"

I looked down at the sand and bit my lip. *Not amazing enough to stay with.*

"You okay?" He tilted his head down to look at me.

"Yeah." I smiled and sniffed. "Just a little sore."

"Of course!" He put the bottle back in its bag

and laid it on the blanket. "Let me help you sit down." He very gently eased me down to the blanket and helped me get comfortable then sat down next to me.

We sat together and watched the waves while he worked up the courage to say whatever it was that he was going to say. Their steady rhythm had been the soundtrack to most of my life. Sometimes, I thought the waves were part of me.

I tried to focus on the moment, to breathe the salt air and feel it in my lungs. To feel *any* air in my lungs. It was a precious commodity that I hadn't appreciated enough.

I grabbed a little handful of sand and let it run through my fingers.

The line of sky closest to the horizon grew dark as the sun started setting behind us.

"You know, Franny, we've been together a while now." Matt's voice was soft enough that I could barely hear it above the waves, and it was thick with emotion. "We've been through some hard times. My dad. All these murders you manage to run into." He looked at me out of the corner of his eye and smiled, but it seemed like a sad smile to me. "Opening the door to that hotel room and seeing— seeing—seeing *that* and seeing you on that bed—

your face was purple, Franny. I thought you were dead. And I—I knew then—I was already planning—"

He turned toward me, but I couldn't look at him. I stared resolutely out to sea, bracing myself for the inevitable. I felt a tear slip out of my eye and roll down my cheek, but I didn't move to brush it away. Matt wiped it with his thumb.

"Will you look at me, Franny?"

I shook my head.

"Okay, then." He moved around and knelt on both knees in front of me, directly in my line of vision.

I looked down at my hands.

He sat back on his heels. "Franny, I don't know what I would have done if I'd lost you that day. I might have—I don't know what I would have done." He closed his eyes and looked down for a minute before looking at me again. "I can't live without you, Franny. I don't want to. You're the best thing that's ever happened to me."

He adjusted his posture so that he was only on one knee. He held out a velvet box and opened it to reveal a sparkling diamond.

I looked up from my hands and met his eyes.

"Francesca Carmella Amaro, will you marry me?"

It took me a long time to process what he'd just asked. It must have felt even longer to him. It certainly felt too long to my coworkers, who were apparently watching from the restaurant patio and started screaming at me to say yes.

"Franny?"

"Oh, Matt," I whispered.

He looked at me with his big, chocolate-brown eyes, so hopeful and so full of love. This was why he'd been nervous. This was why he'd been acting strange.

There was only one thing I could say.

"Absolutely yes."

Recipe 1: Fran's Salad

Ingredients:

- Chicken breasts
- Romaine lettuce, chopped
- Tomatoes, sliced
- Mozzarella, thinly sliced
- Basil
- Croutons
- Olive oil
- Balsamic vinegar

Instructions:

Preheat cast-iron skillet. Season chicken breasts with salt and pepper. Drizzle olive oil on the pan, then sear chicken breasts on both sides until cooked (slightly browned on each side). Slice after cooling.

Assemble lettuce, tomatoes, mozzarella, and basil together in a salad bowl. Add sliced chicken and drizzle with olive oil and balsamic vinegar.

Recipe 2: Fran's Boston Cream Pie with Bourbon

INGREDIENTS:

FOR THE CAKE:

- 2 cups cake flour
- 2 teaspoons baking powder
- 1/2 teaspoon salt
- 1/2 cup unsalted butter at room temperature
- 1 cup granulated sugar
- 3 large eggs
- 1 teaspoon vanilla extract
- 3/4 cup whole milk

For the Filling:

- 1 cup heavy cream
- 2 tablespoons granulated sugar
- 1 tablespoon bourbon
- 1/2 teaspoon vanilla extract
- 2 tablespoons cornstarch
- 2 tablespoons cold water
- 2 large egg yolks, lightly beaten

For the Chocolate Ganache:

- 1 cup semisweet chocolate chips
- 1/2 cup heavy cream
- 2 tablespoons unsalted butter
- 1 tablespoon bourbon

Instructions:

Preheat oven to 350°F. Grease and flour two 9-inch cake pans.

In a medium mixing bowl, whisk together the cake flour, baking powder, and salt. In a large mixing bowl, beat the butter and sugar together until light and fluffy. Beat in the eggs, one at a time, followed by the vanilla extract.

Add the dry ingredients to the wet ingredients in three parts. Divide the batter evenly between the two prepared cake pans and smooth the tops with a spatula. Bake for 25 to 30 minutes or until a toothpick inserted in the center comes out clean. Remove the cakes from the oven and let cool completely on wire racks.

To make the filling, combine the heavy cream, sugar, bourbon, and vanilla extract in a medium saucepan. In a small bowl, whisk together the cornstarch and cold water until smooth. Add the cornstarch mixture to the saucepan and whisk to combine. Whisk in the egg yolks and cook over medium heat, stirring constantly, until the mixture thickens and comes to a boil. Remove from heat and let cool to room temperature. Once the filling has cooled, use a handheld mixer to beat it until it is smooth and creamy. Spread the filling over one of the cake layers and place the other layer on top.

To make the chocolate ganache, place the chocolate chips in a medium heatproof bowl. In a small saucepan, heat the heavy cream and butter over medium heat until just simmering. Pour the hot cream mixture over the chocolate chips and whisk until the chocolate is melted and the mixture is smooth. Stir in the bourbon. Pour the chocolate ganache over the top of the cake, spreading it evenly with a spatula.

Let the cake sit for at least 30 minutes before serving to allow the flavors to meld.

About the Author

Harper Lin is a *USA TODAY* bestselling cozy mystery author. When she's not reading or writing mysteries, she loves going to yoga classes, hiking, and baking with her family and friends.

For a complete list of her books by series, visit her website. Follow Harper on social media using the icons below for the latest insider news.

www.HarperLin.com